ACE G-MAN

THE SUICIDE SQUAD REPORTS FOR DEATH
AND OTHER STORIES

By Emile C. Tepperman

POPULAR PUBLICATIONS • 2022

PUBLISHING HISTORY

"Mr. Zero and the F.B.I. Suicide Squad" originally appeared in the May/June 1939 (Vol. 5, No. 3) issue of *Ace G-Man Stories* magazine. "The Suicide Squad Reports for Death" originally appeared in the July/August 1939 (Vol. 5, No. 4) issue of *Ace G-Man Stories* magazine. "The Suicide Squad's Last Mile" originally appeared in the September/October 1939 (Vol. 6, No. 1) issue of *Ace G-Man Stories* magazine. Copyright 2022 by Argosy Communications, Inc. All rights reserved.

THE SUICIDE SQUAD:
THE SUICIDE SQUAD REPORTS FOR DEATH
AND OTHER STORIES

MR. ZERO AND THE F.B.I.
SUICIDE SQUAD

CHAPTER 1
PRELUDE TO BATTLE

EIGHT PACES up, and eight paces down—Pete Sardis did it a dozen times back and forth, and then stopped, clenched his hands and cursed wildly and profanely. His thick cruel features were twisted into a mask of vindictive but helpless hatred. He was like a vicious cobra whose fangs have been drawn. He seized the bars of his cell door in his two hands and wrenched at them vainly. Then he subsided with a futile sob.

Men in the cells on either side listened to his blistering oaths. Men in the cells opposite watched him with awe. He was a convicted murderer.

Fifteen days ago he had come into Falcon City with two companions, and they had held up a pay-roll messenger. They had machine-gunned the messenger and a guard, had made away with a payroll amounting to one hundred and fifty thousand dollars. The next day they were cornered in an abandoned farmhouse by the state police. His two pals were shot to death. Pete Sardis, with his eyes blinded by tear-gas, had walked out with his hands in the air. But the hundred and fifty thousand dollars of pay-roll loot was never recovered.

Grover Ellis, the district attorney, had rushed the indictment,

1

and Judge Harley, presiding justice of the superior court had given the case precedence on the calendar. Yesterday, Pete Sardis had been convicted of first degree murder. Tomorrow morning he would face Judge Harley for sentence—*"to be hanged by the neck until dead!"*

Plenty of men got away with murder in Falcon City, which was the most corrupt municipality in the Middle West. But Pete Sardis was an outsider, and they were railroading him through to make a showing.

The other prisoners in the county jail knew that he had a hundred and fifty thousand dollars cached away somewhere—small bills that could be easily passed and never identified. But that money was not going to help him. He was going to die.

So they watched him and listened to him—with awe and real interest....

PETE SARDIS flung himself away from the iron bars and threw his heavy body on the narrow cot. He was frightened. He had dealt out death to many a hapless victim, and there had always been a cruel grin on his thick lips when his machine-gun burned out the lives of men. But he couldn't take it. He was going to break up. There were bets being made in the cell block on whether or not he'd collapse before he was sentenced.

Pete Sardis buried his head in his thick hairy arms and sobbed with self-pity. There was nothing he could do about it. He was a rich man, with a hundred and fifty thousand dollars hidden away—and he was going to die.

He jerked his head up as footsteps sounded in the corridor. Two guards were at his door, opening it.

"Come on, you!" one of them ordered. "A visitor."

Sardis gulped. He was meek. He was no longer the blustering murderer. "I—I thought the rules said no visiting-hours after eight?"

"For *this* visitor," the guard grinned, "there are no rules."

They led him downstairs to the interviewing-room. There were little tables, with one chair on either side. A pane of glass bisected the table, rising twelve inches high. You could talk across it, but it would be impossible for a visitor to hand anything to a prisoner.

The eyes of Pete Sardis reflected falling hope when he saw that his visitor was a dark-haired girl. She was thin, and pretty—with long black eyelashes and a soft red mouth. She was nervous.

Pete Sardis slid into the chair facing her. "Who the hell are you?" he asked.

"Call me Miss X," she said, in a low voice. She looked to see if the guard was out of earshot. Then, "You are going to be sentenced to death, Pete Sardis. You are going to hang. That swag you have hidden away isn't going to do you any good."

"Did you come to rub it in?" he snarled.

"No. I came to give you a chance to live!"

Suddenly all the blood drained from the prisoner's face. "You—you can get me outa this?"

"Not I," she said slowly. "But the man who sent me owns this city, and this state. He controls the mayor and the governor and the courts. He can get you off."

"You mean—Mr. Zero?"

Pete Sardis had heard of Mr. Zero, as had every crook in the country. No one knew his identity. But it was a national scandal that Falcon City was in the grip of as vicious a criminal ring as had ever throttled a community.

"You should have known better," the girl said calmly, "than to have come here to do a job like that pay-roll robbery—without making a connection first."

Pete Sardis lowered his eyes. "I guess you're right. But we figured we'd get in and out before the cops could lay a hand on us."

"Well," she asked, "do you want to beat this rap?"

"How can I? I've been convicted."

"Under the law of this state, it is within the discretion of the judge to set aside the jury's verdict before sentence is imposed."

A gleam of hope entered the prisoner's eyes. But it quickly died. "Judge Harley would never do that. It would make an awful stink. He'd be impeached."

The girl smiled faintly. "Judge Harley will do it—if Mr. Zero tells him to. But it will cost you one hundred and fifty thousand dollars. You don't have to trust me. If you agree, you will go free tomorrow. As soon as you are free, you must go and get that swag from the place where you have it hidden, and turn it over to me."

"It—it'll leave me broke," Pete Sardis faltered.

"Better to be broke than dead."

"There's something else," he said. "There's a G-man coming from Washington to question me in the morning. They want to ask me about a couple jobs that me and the boys done in other states. He's got a warrant, too. If I'm let outa here, he'll take me to the federal court—"

5

"The G-man will also be taken are of," the girl said. "There will be no extra charge for that…."

TWO HOURS later, the phone in Judge Victor Harley's home rang insistently. His wife put down her knitting to answer it, but the judge stopped her. What he said was, "I'll take it, Emma."

Judge Victor Harley was a lean man of fifty with a high fore-head and deeply sunken, pallid cheeks. In his lusterless eyes there lurked the shadow of some great tragedy. And his wife's listless demeanor indicated that she shared his suffering. She watched him almost breathlessly as he picked up the phone.

A sharp, metallic voice spoke out of the receiver. "This is Mr. Zero."

Judge Harley's knuckles whitened as he gripped the instrument. "What—what do you want now?"

"A small matter, Judge. A favor which it will be very easy for you to do. Pete Sardis appears before you in the morning. Instead of sentencing him, you will state that you feel the verdict was based upon insufficient evidence—and you will set the verdict aside and discharge the defendant!"

"I won't do it. Damn you, I won't do it—"

Judge Harley broke off. There was a click at the other end. He was talking into a dead line. He put the phone down, and stared across the room at his wife. "You heard?"

Emma Harley nodded wordlessly. The voice had been loud enough to carry across to her. "You must do it, Victor. There is no other way."

"It will mean the end, Emma. I will have to resign."

6

"Perhaps then he will have no further use for you. Perhaps he will give us back—"

Her voice broke on a choking sob. "No, no. He is too cruel, that Mr. Zero. He means to turn the knife in our hearts!"

Victor Harley came and put an arm around his wife. "There is one hope," he said softly. "A G-man is coming in the morning, to question Sardis. I have spoken to Washington on the phone. They are sending the G-man to see me in my chambers in court. Perhaps if I tell this man everything, he can help us."

"If he ever gets here," she broke in.

AT SEVEN minutes after nine the next morning, the train from Washington pulled into Central Station at the north end of Falcon City. A curly-haired, eager-eyed young man hurried from the train, carrying a briefcase. He went through the station, and entered one of the waiting cabs at the curb.

"I want to go to the superior court," he told the driver.

"Okay," said the cabby, and started the car. As they pulled out, a limousine fell into line behind them.

The cab moved slowly. Suddenly both doors were jerked open, and two men sprang into the cab, crowding against the curly-haired passenger. They both had guns, which they thrust into the young man's ribs.

"Just sit still!" one of them grated.

The young man started to go for a gun in his shoulder holster. The gunman on the right reversed his gun and hit him hard behind the ear. The young man slumped in the seat.

The other gunman covered the driver. "Keep going, pal. Don't look around!"

The driver was white-faced. He kept going. Twice the gunmen told him where to turn, and he obeyed. The limousine continued to follow them.

In ten minutes they reached an outlying section, where there were few houses. They opened the left-hand door of the cab and bundled the unconscious young G-man out into the gutter. He rolled over twice, and lay still.

One of the two gunmen, who had a cast in his left eye, leaned out and signaled to the limousine behind. The limousine put on a burst of speed, accelerated to fifty, and ran over the body of the G-man. The driver directed his car in such a way that the heavy tires struck the unconscious man's neck.

Then the cab and the limousine disappeared.

THERE WERE beads of sweat on Judge Victor Harley's high, scholarly forehead. Attired in his judicial robes, he was pacing the floor of his small office in the superior court building, in much the same fashion that Pete Sardis had paced the floor of his cell last night.

A dozen times he glanced at his wrist watch. It was twenty-seven minutes after nine. His telephone rang. He picked it up with a trembling hand.

That same metallic voice crackled in his ear. "Before opening court, Judge, I suggest that you tune in on WAFC at once. It will settle any doubts there may be in your mind."

Again the phone clicked dead.

Automatically, the judge turned the dial of his small radio to WAFC, the Municipal Broadcasting Station of Falcon City. The announcer was saying, "Flash! A man has been found dead on

High Street, with a broken neck. He was apparently a victim of a hit-and-run driver. There were no witnesses of the accident. The victim has been identified as James Reynolds, a Special Agent of the Federal Bureau of Investigation. Mayor Devore regrets this accident deeply, as it is the third fatality to Federal G-men in recent weeks. The climate of Falcon City seems to be very unhealthy for G-men.

"Since this was clearly an accident, there will be no investigation. Mayor Devore has already notified F.B.I. headquarters in Washington, but he has warned the Director that he does not want federal men in this city unless they are here on legitimate business. We are well able to administer the law in this city, and the Constitution of the United States protects us against having our rights and authority usurped by federal bureaus...."

Long before the announcer finished, Judge Victor Harley had left his office. With sagging shoulders he ascended the bench and faced a crowded courtroom and a smirking defendant.

"Peter Sardis," he said, "I have examined your case carefully. I find that the verdict of guilty brought in by the jury was based upon insufficient evidence. Therefore, under power vested in this court by statute, I hereby set aside the said verdict and discharge you from the jurisdiction of this court...."

CHAPTER 2
F.B.I. SUICIDE SQUAD

FOR SEVERAL years there have been rumors around Washington that the F.B.I. has a Suicide Squad—a group

9

of men who have no regular duties, but who wait for the one inevitable assignment from which there will be no return.

People have wondered just what kind of men comprise this Suicide Squad—and why.

Certainly, the three men who now sat in the private office of the Director would have been the first to deny the rumors—if asked.

Six months ago there had been five of them. Two months ago there were four. Now there were only three—Kerrigan and Murdoch and Klaw.

Johnny Kerrigan was a big blond, with a pair of dancing blue eyes, and shoulders like a stevedore's. Dan Murdoch was tall and black-haired and black-eyed and thin-lipped. He moved with the effortless ease of a jungle beast, and was just as dangerous. Stephen Klaw was small, compared to the other two. Only five feet seven-and-a-half, he was slim and wiry. Because of that, one might take him for a kid—were it not for the curious gleam in his slate-grey eyes. Many men had, to their sorrow, made the mistake of underestimating him.

So there they were—Kerrigan and Murdoch and Klaw. And there was one quality common to all of them—the quality of hard-bitten, headstrong willfulness which had wrecked their chances of advancement with the F.B.I.

Johnny Kerrigan had punched a senator's son in the nose in a barroom fight. Dan Murdoch had shot a croupier to death in a crooked gambling house. Steve Klaw had told the chairman of a Congressional investigating committee to go to hell, because he didn't like the tone in which he was questioned as to why he had shot to kill in a gunfight with three bandits, instead of trying to capture them.

Any other three men who had done similar misdeeds would have found themselves out in the cold. But Kerrigan and Murdoch and Klaw had records which few men could equal. It would have been impossible to explain to a hero-loving public just why they had been discharged from the service.

The Director was looking for an excuse to keep then on the payroll, and he was glad to be able to tell certain powers that be that it would be undiplomatic to oust Kerrigan and Murdoch and Klaw. But he had to promise that he would use them only in emergencies, and never for routine duties where they might hurt the noses or the feelings of other powers that be.

So he gave them cases that looked impossible, or that looked as if certain death was waiting at the other end. This was one of those cases.

"You three men are going to Falcon City," he told them.

"Aha!" said Johnny Kerrigan. "Into the jaws of death!"

"It amounts to that." The Director spoke soberly. "They're killing our men off, one by one. And they do it so cleverly that it looks like accident. They don't give us an excuse to go in there in force. If I sent thirty or forty men in there on the present evidence, they'd raise a howl to Congress that we are violating the sanctity of local state government. And if I send one or two men, they'll kill them—like young Reynolds this morning!"

Dan Murdoch grinned thinly. "So Kerrigan and Murdoch and Klaw go into Falcon City and rip things wide open!"

"Exactly," was the answer. "You three hellions can do it if

anyone can. Officially, I'm sending you there to arrest Pete Sardis—to serve the warrant that Reynolds had for him. Unofficially, I want the power of Mr. Zero broken. He's running that city to suit his own vicious taste. He's brought in thugs from the underworlds of a dozen cities, and appointed them police officers. He runs slot machines and gambling establishments, and drug and white-slave dives. He has flagrantly flaunted his power in our faces. Hundreds of law-abiding citizens have written begging us to do something about it. But our hands are tied unless we can prove overt violation of a Federal statute."

"If one of us gets killed publicly and openly," Stephen Klaw broke in, speaking in his soft drawl which was belied by the slate-hardness of his gray eyes, "that would be good cause for the F.B.I. to go in there!"

"I hope none of you will get killed," said the Director. "But it'll be a miracle if you all come out of it alive. Mr. Zero is diabolically clever."

"One of us," Stephen Klaw mused, "would have to go there alone, and openly, to sort of draw Mr. Zero's fire. The other two could be working under cover in the meanwhile."

"You will remember," said the Director, "that if you do anything out of line, you will be disowned. And if you prefer not to take the assignment, I will withdraw it."

"Not a chance!" boomed Johnny Kerrigan. "We've been warming our pants long enough. This is what we've been waiting for!"

The Director smiled, almost with fondness. "At least one of

you won't come back from this job," he said. "I—I wish I didn't have to send you."

Kerrigan and Murdoch and Klaw shook hands with him solemnly, and filed out of the office. Once in the corridor, they let out a wild *"Whoop!"*

Little Stephen Klaw said, "Look, the guy who goes there alone will be the bait. The weaker looking he is, the better. I guess I fill the bill—"

"Nix!" barked Johnny Kerrigan. "We toss. Odd man goes in alone."

Dan Murdoch nodded. They took out coins and tossed. Kerrigan and Murdoch got heads. Steve Klaw got a tail. He grinned.

They walked silently out of the building and went to the parking-space where Dan Murdoch's car was sitting. He got a bottle and three paper cups out of the side pocket, and filled them with rye. Then they all touched cups and drank.

"See you in Hell, boys," said Stephen Klaw.

"See you in Hell, Shrimp," echoed Kerrigan and Murdoch.

Stephen Klaw raised his hand in mock salute, and turned and walked away.

In front of the Department of Justice Building he encountered newspapermen.

"Here's an item for you, boys," he said. "Stephen Klaw, Special Agent of the Federal Bureau of Investigation, has been assigned to go to Falcon City and find Pete Sardis. I am instructed to continue the investigation which Special Agent Reynolds was prevented from completing, due to his unfortunate accident. I am taking the five-fifteen train, and will arrive in Falcon City at eleven-forty-nine tonight." He paused, then added, "And you can say that I'll be wearing a white gardenia in my lapel—to make it easy to identify me!"

CHAPTER 3
DATE WITH DEATH

AT ELEVEN-FORTY-NINE, Stephen Klaw alighted from the Washington train at Central Station in Falcon City. True to his promise, he was wearing a white gardenia in his buttonhole. Unlike young Reynolds, he did not carry a brief-case. He sauntered carelessly out into the street, with his hands deep in his coat pockets, and apparently without a care in the world. He got into a taxicab.

"Do you know where Judge Victor Harley lives?" he asked the driver. "I mean the judge that set this Pete Sardis free."

The driver nodded. "Yeah. On High Street."

"All right, that's where I want to go."

The cab started.

Looking through the rear window, Steve Klaw saw that a long black limousine had pulled out from the curb and was crawling behind them.

He was startled by the noise of the opening of both his cab doors, and turned to see that two men with guns in their hands were crowding in on either side of him. One of the men had a cast in the left eye.

"Just sit still!" this one grated.

Steve Klaw sat still. The other gunman poked his revolver into the back of the taxi driver's neck.

"Drive straight ahead," he ordered. "And don't look around."

Steve Klaw smiled faintly. "How's it going to be this time, pal?" he asked. "The same as with Reynolds? Found dead on the street?"

The man with the cast grinned. "We never tell the same joke twice, guy. This time you're going over the bridge. You were a sucker to come here."

"Tell me one thing before I kick the bucket," Steve begged. "Who is Mr. Zero?"

The man with the cast in his eye laughed out loud. "Hear that, Louie? He wants to know who is Mr. Zero!"

Louie attended strictly to the business of keeping the driver covered. He grunted.

"Wise guy! You don't seem to be worried, Mr. G-man. Ain't you got no imagination? How'll it feel at the bottom of the river?"

"I'm not there yet," Steve said slowly.

At Louie's direction, the quaking cab-driver swung east over the North End Bridge. They came to a place where the W.P.A. was repairing the roadbed. The side rails of the bridge had been temporarily removed.

"We get out here," said the man with the cast.

"I won't go," said Steve.

"Too bad, pal," said the man with the cast. He reversed his gun and raised it to strike Steve behind the ear, while Louie turned to keep him covered.

Stephen Klaw fired the automatic in his right hand pocket and the automatic in his left hand pocket simultaneously. He shot through the cloth without aiming very much, but he shot each gun three times quickly.

All three slugs from the left-hand gun tore into the abdomen of the man with the cast in his left eye. The pellets from the right-hand gun hit Louie in various places, one of which was over the heart.

The cab driver leaped out of his seat and ran away with fear pistoning his legs.

Stephen Klaw clambered swiftly over the body of Louie, and leaped to the roadbed just as the limousine came abreast of him.

There was only one man in the limousine, at the wheel. He had a gun in his hand, but he was hampered in using it by reason of having to hold the wheel with one hand. Stephen Klaw shot him in the head.

The limousine swerved sharply as the man slumped, and cut across the bridge at a sharp angle. It hit the guard rail and came to a stop.

Steve looked inside the taxicab. The man with the cast in his eye was not dead yet. But he was unconscious, and there was little chance that he would live till he could get to a hospital.

Steve Klaw smiled grimly and turned and walked back toward the city end of the bridge. Twice he stepped into the shadow of a girder as police cars with screaming sirens raced past him. He got over without being stopped and found a second-hand clothing store down near the river front, where he bought a new jacket to match his trousers. He threw the old jacket into a trash barrel after removing all identifying tags.

Then he took another cab and went to the Falcon City Hotel in the heart of town. He entered a telephone booth in the lobby and called the Falcon City Broadcasting Station—WAFC.

"Please announce," he said to the person who answered the phone, "that Stephen Klaw, Special Agent of the Federal Bureau of Investigation, is still alive, and that he is now in the Falcon City Hotel, awaiting the next move of Mr. Zero. Convey my compliments to Mr. Zero, and tell him that I wish him better luck next time!"

He hung up before the startled recipient of the message could throw further questions at him.

He inserted another nickel in the slot, and called Judge Harley's home. "This is Stephen Klaw, Special Agent of the F.B.I.," he said. "I am here in place of Agent Reynolds, who was killed this morning. I understand you wished to make a statement."

"I am sorry, Mr. Klaw," Judge Harley interrupted. "I have nothing to say!"

Steve's eyes narrowed. "You have changed your mind about asking assistance from the F.B.I.?"

"Yes."

"Can you tell me the real reason why you freed Pete Sardis this morning?"

"No," said the judge.

"Did you do it at the order of Mr. Zero?" Klaw asked.

"I have nothing to say." There was a click as Judge Harley hung up.

Stephen Klaw came out of the telephone booth thoughtfully, fingering the gardenia in his buttonhole. He purchased a copy of the *Falcon City Evening News*. There was a headline that caught his eye at once:

F.B.I. SENDS PROFESSIONAL
KILLER TO FALCON CITY

Stephen Klaw, who has already been under investigation for his murderous deadliness with guns, is on his way to Falcon City with a gardenia in his lapel....

Steve grinned at that, and glanced at another headline:

DISTRICT ATTORNEY ELLIS DEMANDS
IMPEACHMENT OF JUDGE HARLEY

STEPHEN KLAW crumpled the paper and dropped it in a waste-paper basket. He crossed the lobby and entered the Hotel Grille through the side door. This was a spacious dining-room where the elite of the city came at night.

Several people at the tables looked at him curiously, eyeing the gardenia. He allowed the headwaiter to seat him at a table near the dance floor.

"Just one in your party, sir?"

"No," said Steve. "I'm expecting company."

"A lady?"

"I doubt it. I'm expecting to hear from—Mr. Zero!"

The headwaiter's face became pale. "I—I don't know what you mean, sir."

"Never mind. Bring me rye whiskey in an *unopened* bottle," said Steve.

"A bottle, sir?"

"And unopened. I don't like knockout drops in my drinks."

The man grew frigid. "That's an insult—"

He stopped at the sudden cold gleam in Stephen Klaw's gray eyes. His voice trailed away.

"Y-yes, sir. An unopened bottle." He hurried away.

There was a hard-jawed, powerfully built man sitting with a party of six at a near-by table. This man was watching Steve with a frown. He excused himself to the others at his table and got up and came over quietly to where Steve was sitting.

"Do you mind if I sit down for a moment? I am District Attorney Grover Ellis."

Stephen Klaw nodded.

Ellis seated himself. His eyes bored into Stephen Klaw's, then dropped to the gardenia. "You are the G-man who announced your arrival in the newspapers."

Steve inclined his head, but said nothing.

Ellis went on, frowning. "You're mad, Klaw. I wouldn't give a nickel for your life. Mr. Zero will get you. And you can't get him. I know—I've tried for three years. He only lets me live because he needs a little opposition for the sake of publicity. And I can't hurt him much. Even when I convict a murderer like Sardis, he gets him off. But you—you are deliberately challenging his power in the city. If you stay alive, all his thugs and gunmen will lose respect for him. I'm surprised he hasn't tried already—"

"He's made one try," Stephen Klaw said. "I'm waiting for the next."

"Damn it, man!" Ellis exploded. "What are you trying to accomplish?"

"I'm trying to get myself killed in a spectacular way," Steve told him. "With plenty of witnesses to prove it wasn't an accident. So the F.B.I. can come in here and really go to town."

"My God!" said Ellis. Then he recovered himself. "Mr. Zero won't play into your hands like that. He'll get you the way he got the others the way he does everything else in Falcon City. It's suicide. You're throwing your life away."

"It's my life, Mr. Ellis."

The district attorney grew red in the face and pushed up from the chair. "You're a hard man to try to help, Klaw!"

"I'm not asking you for help."

District Attorney Ellis shrugged his shoulders, and left the table.

Stephen Klaw glanced at his wristwatch. It was fifteen minutes since he had phoned the broadcasting station. Plenty of time for Mr. Zero to have received the news, and to make another attempt. He sipped his rye highball, keeping one eye on the door.

A girl came into the dining-room, and stopped just inside the doorway. She wore a finely tailored blue suit which set off her slender figure excellently. She had long black lashes, and a soft red mouth. There was a queer expression in her eyes—perhaps fear, perhaps nervousness.

She saw the gardenia in Steve's lapel, and came directly to his table, slipped into the chair which Ellis had just vacated.

"You're looking for Pete Sardis," she said without preamble.

Stephen Klaw studied her for a full minute. "Do you know where he is?"

She nodded jerkily. "I'll take you there."

Steve grinned slowly. "Did Mr. Zero send you? Are you going to lead me into a trap?"

"Yes!"

She was outwardly cool. But Steve detected a slight trembling of the slim hand which held the purse at her breast. She went on hurriedly, speaking so low that he barely caught the words.

"We are being watched by a dozen people who would gladly report everything I'm saying, to Mr. Zero. He has made plans to get you, in one way or another. If those men failed at the station, I was to come here and lure you to your death, using Pete Sardis as the bait. I have done Mr. Zero's contact work for months now. I am the one who made the proposition to Sardis, in jail. God forgive me, I have done other terrible things at Mr. Zero's orders. But I'm through. I won't take you to your death. Refuse. Refuse to come with me."

Steve Klaw smiled. "You expect me to believe that you have suddenly changed sides?"

"No, no. It isn't that," she said. "I dared not refuse to work for Mr. Zero. Just as Judge Harley dared not refuse to discharge Pete Sardis. But I have never helped him to do murder. This—this will be murder. If you come to the place where Sardis is, you will surely die, and it will be murder!"

"That's what I want," said Stephen Klaw.

"You don't understand," the girl argued. "You'll be found dead somehow, but there'll be no proof that it was murder."

"How?" Klaw asked.

"I—I don't know. He never takes me into his confidence."

"Who is Mr. Zero?" he insisted.

"I don't know that either. I get my orders over the phone." She halted.

"What hold has he over you?" Klaw asked now.

"My brother—George Payne—is in the death house in the County Jail. He was framed for a murder he never committed. Judge Harley has been postponing the date for sentence. Each month he sets it ahead for thirty days. If I should disobey Mr. Zero, my brother will hang."

"I see," said Stephen Klaw, softly. He got to his feet. There was an unholy glitter in his eyes. "Take me to Pete Sardis."

"But it's a trap. You'll *die*—"

"Take me to Pete Sardis!" he repeated harshly.

CHAPTER 4
G-MEN ASK FOR IT!

A T ABOUT the time when Stephen Klaw was ordering his rye and ginger ale in the dining-room of the Falcon City Hotel, two disreputable-looking characters might have

Chapter Thirty

Clint knocked on the office door, and Josephine called out, "Come on in."

As he entered, he saw her seated behind a desk.

"Ah, you brought your beer with you," she commented. "I was going to offer you a brandy."

"That's okay," Clint said. "I prefer a beer."

"Then I'll get you another one. Have a seat."

Josephine went to the door and shouted for the bartender to bring a cold beer."

She returned to her desk, stopping first to pour herself a glass of brandy.

"Why do I get the feeling you didn't come here for a free drink, or to see me?" Josephine asked.

"I'm sorry, Josephine," Clint said, "but I did have to send a telegram."

"And one of great importance, I'll bet."

"That's true," Clint said, "but I can't say I wasn't looking forward to seeing you again."

She smiled and said, "And I, you. Will you be waiting in town for your reply?"

"I'm afraid not," Clint said. "I have lots of work to do, but I will be returning for the reply very soon."

"That's a shame," she said. "I was hoping we would have time to get to know each other better . . . much better."

"That's something I would've liked, as well."

"And how is your mine?" she asked. "Flourishing?"

"I'm not ready to talk about that, yet," Clint said.

"As close-mouthed as ever, eh?" she asked. "Not ready for investors yet?"

"Not nearly," he said. "We don't even know what we have."

"Are you east of town, as most of the mines are?" she asked.

"I really can't say."

"Well, then," she said, "maybe you just don't want to talk."

"I can think of many things to do with someone as beautiful as you, other than talk."

"Do you see that door?" She pointed to a door in the back of the small office. "I sleep in a bed behind that door very often."

She stood up and walked around the desk to him. He came to his feet, set his beer down, and took her hands.

"But I can think of things to do with you other than sleep."

"And I'm sure we have the same things in mind."

They came together in a long, passionate kiss that punctuated their words, and continued as they went through that door.

On the other side was a large room with a big bed. Josephine could have used that room many times for other than sleeping, but Clint didn't think twice about that. He was satisfied with the fact that she was about to use it with him, now.

There was no rush behind what they were doing, although there was a bit of urgency as more and more of their clothes came off.

She didn't blink when he hung his gunbelt on the bedpost. They peeled clothing off each other until they were both naked. She was a full-bodied woman, with large heavy breasts and wide hips. He took her breasts in his hands, cradled them there, enjoying the way the undersides filled his palms, and the way she moaned and bit her lips when he pinched her large, brown nipples.

She reached between them to take his large, hard cock in her hands, stroking it until it was even harder and fuller, and then they tumbled onto the bed together, arms and legs entangled.

She glided down his body, running her hands and lips over his skin. He wondered about her when he met her in the general store, but he never imagined this would happen. He thought there would be no time for this.

He was as relaxed as he could be, while still aware of his surroundings and where his gun was. As she climbed atop him and took his hard cock into the depths of her hot, wet pussy, he wished he could give himself up completely to the sensations he was experiencing. But in his life, there was always the possibility that someone was lurking behind a door, or outside a window, with a gun. The only time he could really relax was when he was in the presence of a friend like Talbot Roper, John Locke or Bat Masterson. Those were literally the only people he believed would never turn on him.

He didn't know Josephine well, and had no way of knowing if this was her way of gaining control of him. To show her it wasn't the case, he grabbed her, flipped her onto her back and speared her, driving his cock as deep and as hard as he could, as fast as he could. The cries that emanated from her were ones of pure pleasure, not a single one of alarm at a plan going wrong.

He assumed that things were going exactly the way she had planned when she invited him here.

been seen near the residence of Judge Victor Harley on High Street.

Their clothes were wrinkled and dirty, and they had a stubble of beard on their faces. But the car which they parked around the corner on Clay Street had a powerful eight-cylinder motor which could do ninety without trouble. It is doubtful if anyone who did not know them well would have been able to recognize big Johnny Kerrigan and Dan Murdoch in these two bleary-eyed stumble bums.

They had tapped the telephone wire in the judge's house, and were going to take turns at sitting with the earphones in the cellar.

Dan Murdoch was just getting out of the car when his hand froze on the door handle. A long seven-passenger car was pulling up at the door of the judge's house, around the corner. And at the same instant, Judge Harley and his wife emerged from the house.

Murdoch's eyes narrowed as he saw them enter the car. "Do you see what I see, Johnny?"

There were two men in that limousine, one at the wheel and the other in the rear. The man in the rear was adjusting a blindfold bandage to the judge's eyes. He finished, and then turned to do the same for Emma Harley.

"This is the break, Dan!" exclaimed Johnny Kerrigan. "We'll tail them."

"If those muggs are taking Harley and his wife anywhere, they wouldn't be dumb enough to let anyone stick on their tail," was the answer. "I'll ride with them. You follow my flash."

23

Kerrigan nodded. This was a trick they had tried several times in the past. Though dangerous, it had often succeeded.

Murdoch slipped away and sidled around the corner, keeping on the blind side of the limousine. Just as it began to pull away from the curb, he stepped up on the rear bumper, and got hold of the spare tire with one hand. He rode that limousine just the way street kids will steal a ride on the back of a passing car.

Kerrigan waited till the limousine was a block away, then swung in after them. He let them gain another block before he switched on his lights.

The trail led through unfrequented portions of the city. Twice Kerrigan almost lost them, but each time he caught the flicker of Murdoch's flashlight as the limousine turned a corner far ahead. He realized the wisdom of Murdoch's decision to ride with them. The driver of that car was deliberately twisting and turning in order to lose any possible tails. At last the man was apparently convinced that he was not being followed, for he swung into Eastern Boulevard and headed out of town.

Kerrigan remained almost a quarter of a mile behind, guided by Murdoch's flashlight. They drove that way for thirty minutes. Then the limousine swung into a private driveway leading up to a low, rambling stucco structure set far back from the road.

Kerrigan parked his car and walked up toward the house. He got a glimpse of the door being opened by a huge, hulking man, dressed like an interne in white trousers and jacket, and with a short club hanging by a thong from his wrist. The judge and his wife, still blindfolded, were led into the house by the two men who had brought them here, and then the door closed, shutting off the little light that had been cast on the driveway.

Kerrigan moved more quickly now. He saw Murdoch come out of the shadow of the limousine, which had been left in front of the door. They moved up close to the porch, and saw that there was a small metal plaque alongside the door:

DOCTOR RUNCIE'S PRIVATE SANITARIUM

Murdoch and Kerrigan moved around to the side of the house. All the windows were heavily barred. They were ten or twelve feet above the ground, so that it was impossible to look inside.

Murdoch was a little in advance of Kerrigan, and he stepped around toward the rear of the house. Abruptly a shadow appeared before him. It was the figure of a man with a rifle.

"Where do you think you're going, bozo?"

Murdoch said, "Want to make something of it, guy?" and moved deliberately in toward the muzzle of the rifle.

The guard raised the gun. "Don't move or I'll give it to you in the guts—"

He broke off short as the huge figure of Johnny Kerrigan came hurtling in at him from the side. Before he could fire he was sent sprawling, with Johnny on top of him. Johnny smashed a right and a left down into the man's face. His head bounced against the concrete walk, and he lay still.

Kerrigan got up and dusted his hands.

Murdoch patted him on the back. "Nice teamwork, Johnny."

Kerrigan grunted. "We can leave him. I don't think he'll be getting up for a while."

He pointed to a window in the rear of the building, where a man was pulling down a shade. It was one of the men from the limousine.

THEY FOLLOWED the concrete walk till they got under the window. Kerrigan clasped his two hands together, and held them waist high. Murdoch stepped up on them, and his head came level with the window.

There was a crack about a half inch wide where the shade didn't come all the way down, and he could peer inside.

Judge Harley and his wife were in there, without the blindfolds. They were both kneeling beside a cot upon which lay a pallid girl of about seventeen. It was easy to see that she must once have been beautiful. But now her cheeks were sunken, and dark were circles under her eyes. She wore a white flannel hospital nightgown which exposed her arms. Murdoch saw dozens of tiny needle pricks on her left arm from elbow to shoulder.

The two men from the limousine were standing on either side of the door, with guns in their hands.

Judge Harley was dry-eyed as he knelt beside the cot. But Emma Harley's body was wracked by short, jerking sobs. She threw her arms around the pallid patient on the cot, and buried her head on the girl's breast.

The girl raised a hand which was thin almost to transparency, and stroked Mrs. Harley's hair.

Murdoch could see her lips slowly forming words, "Take me home, mother—please take me home."

Mrs. Harley screamed with pent-up emotion, and sprang away from the cot. She swung on the two guards at the door. Her voice was so loud now, that Murdoch could plainly hear her.

"You devils, you can't keep her here any longer!"

One of the two men snarled something, and stepped forward and slapped her hard across the face with the back of his hand. She fell back across the cot from the force of the blow.

Judge Harley, his face livid with fury, sprang to his feet and started toward the gunman. The fellow sneered and brought his gun up to cover the judge.

Dan Murdoch had seen enough. He called down, "Don't drop me now, Johnny," and drew his revolver. He raked it across the narrow strip of exposed window between two of the bars, shattering the glass. He stuck his fingers in through the aperture and yanked at the shade. It rattled all the way up on its roller.

The two gunmen were momentarily startled into immobility. But when they saw Murdoch's grinning face in the window, they started to shoot. Their aim was spoiled by their haste, and they didn't get the chance to fire again.

Murdoch pulled his trigger twice, with cold deliberation. That cold grin remained fixed on Dan Murdoch's dark handsome face as the two hoods went crashing back into the door—one with a ball in his heart, the other with blood spurting from a torn throat.

From somewhere in the hallway beyond the closed door a hoarse shout echoed the reverberating din of the gunfire. The bodies of the two gunmen were shoved aside as the door was thrust open. The big white-coated man with the club came barging in.

Murdoch covered him from the window, and said, "Stand still, boy-friend!"

The man's face went white when he saw that killer's grin on Murdoch's lips. Slowly he raised his hands in the air, with the club swinging from his right wrist.

"If you want to get your daughter out of here, Judge," said Murdoch, "pick up a gun and cover that baby."

Judge Harley, still a little dazed, got one of the revolvers dropped by the gunmen and pointed it at the big man.

"I'll keep him covered all right," he said savagely. "I only hope he tries to escape. He's one of the men who tortured my daughter!"

"We're coming in the front way," Murdoch told him. Then he said to Kerrigan, "Okay, Johnny."

Kerrigan lowered him to the ground. They started toward the front of the house, and suddenly they heard the sound of a motor racing. They broke into a run and got around in front in time to see a small coupé tear down the driveway and swing into the road heading back toward the city.

"Some one's making a break!" Murdoch exclaimed.

Johnny Kerrigan gave him a little push. "Go after them, Dan. I'll handle this!"

MURDOCH LEAPED into the limousine in front of the door. He jammed the starter down, got in first and raced her down to the road, taking the curve at the foot of the driveway on two wheels.

28

He kept his foot all the way down to the floorboards, and the big car ate up the road, the speedometer moving to seventy-five, eighty, eighty-five.

He caught sight of the two red taillights of the little coupé, and began to overhaul it rapidly. Grimly he took out his gun and put it on the seat beside him. Slowly but surely he began to pull abreast of the coupé.

There was only one man in the fugitive car. He was stout and ball-headed, and there was terror in the face that he turned as Kerrigan came abreast of him.

Johnny picked up the gun and waved it in signal for the fat man to pull over. The fat man obeyed.

Johnny swung his limousine in front of the coupé, and got out. He came around and yanked open the door of the coupé and put a big paw on the fat man's collar. He pulled him out bodily.

"And who might *you* be, my fat friend?" he asked, almost gently.

"I—I'm Doctor Runcie. What—what is the meaning of this?"

Johnny Kerrigan grinned. *"You* tell *me.* And talk very fast, my fat friend."

Runcie tried to bluster some more. "This is an outrage! I don't understand!"

Kerrigan's eyes were dancing points of fire. He smashed a fist into Runcie's mouth. "I said to talk. I mean talk *sense!"*

Runcie bounced back with Johnny's blow. Then he cowered as Johnny raised a fist again. "Wait! Wait! I'll talk. I—I thought you were—were robbers, so I escaped."

Kerrigan hit him again.

He went down to the ground, moaning.

Kerrigan picked him up by the collar, held him dangling off the ground. "Want more?"

"No, no! God, no! What—what do you want me to tell you?"

"You were holding that girl back there at Mr. Zero's orders. Who's Mr. Zero?"

"God, I don't know," said the doctor. "I get my orders by phone."

"Suppose you had to get in touch with Mr. Zero in a hurry? What would you do?" The G-man waited.

"I'd call that girl."

"What girl?"

"I don't know her name. I just have her telephone number. It's Falcon Two-four-one-four-o."

"I see," said Johnny Kerrigan.

CHAPTER 5
GIRLS MEAN TROUBLE

THE GIRL parked her cat on Pitt Street, in front of a remodeled brownstone. "This is where Pete Sardis is hiding," she said to Stephen Klaw. "Apartment Four-B, on the top floor, in the rear. Pete Sardis is up there."

"Ah," said Stephen Klaw.

His eyes were busy searching the shadows on either side of the street. He saw nothing. There was a car parked about fifty feet away, on the opposite side. From here it looked unoccupied. But there might be men in it, out of sight. There were dark doorways on either side of the street. Men might be lurking there. Mister Zero would be sure to give Pete Sardis reinforcements for his job.

He turned and saw the girl looking at him intently.

"If you go up there, Mr. Klaw, you're going to your death," she said. "Why don't you get the local police to help you?"

He smiled faintly. "And have some of Mr. Zero's boys right with me when I go up? Thank you for the suggestion. I'll be safer alone."

She shrugged. "I told Mr. Zero that I wouldn't bring you here without warning you that it was a trap. He said it would be quiet all right. He said he was certain you would choose to come alone."

"Thank you for that, too," said Stephen Klaw. "And now, if you will forgive me, I must do a very unpleasant thing."

He took handcuffs from his pocket, and snapped them around her wrists, running the links through a spoke of the steering wheel.

"Just so you'll be here when I come back," he explained. "If I don't come back, it'll be simple for Mr. Zero's boys to take the key from my pocket and release you."

She offered no resistance. "You're a hard man, Stephen Klaw."

Then as he climbed from the car, she spoke again, softly—so softly that he almost did not hear it. "I—I wish you luck!"

He nodded, and walked away from the car, directly toward the entrance of the brownstone. He walked with his hands deep in his jacket pockets, almost with a slouch—so that he seemed barely more than a kid. But there was that curious gleam in his slate-gray eyes, and he was missing nothing that was to be seen on the street. For instance, he saw the limousine that turned the far corner, slowly, and came to a stop almost at once. As it passed for a moment under the street light, he recognized that it was the same make and year as the one in which he was to have been sent hurtling over the bridge tonight.

His lips tightened. Mr. Zero was making sure that his escape would be cut off.

He did not stop. He put his hand on the door knob and thrust it open, and stepped into the vestibule. He tried the vestibule door, and found it unlocked. They were making it easy for him.

He stepped into the hall. There was a soft light here. The staircase was directly ahead. He could not see into the shadows behind it, neither could he see what was on the first floor landing.

He took out his flashlight and sent its beam lancing upward. There was no one on the stairs. He sent the light into the shadows behind the stairs. There was nothing there.

He held the flashlight in his left hand, and kept the right buried in his pocket. Firmly, without attempting to deaden the sound of his steps, he started to mount the stairs. Each step might presage a burst of machine-gun fire. And then again, they might let him reach the top.

He reached the first-floor landing without opposition. Now came the next test. He must cross that hall to the next flight of stairs. And while he crossed, the door of the apartment behind him might open and spew death.

He walked here on the balls of his feet, lightly, so that the sound of an opening door would be sure to reach him. But there was nothing.

He used his flashlight once more, and began to mount the second flight.

Suddenly he stopped dead. A sound reached him—the sound of a foot scraping the floor on the next landing.

At the same instant he heard another sound below him. The door of the front apartment on the first floor was being cautiously opened.

His eyes gleamed. He was to be caught between two fires here. If he tried to go up, the gunner on the next landing would get him. If he tried to go down, the gunner on the first floor would get him.

Suddenly a powerful flashlight from the next landing clicked on, bathing him in merciless light.

Stephen Klaw acted almost before that flashlight focused. He dropped his own light. His right hand came up with an automatic, and began to trigger shots upward. His left dived into the pocket and came out with the other gun.

His swift shots thundered in the hall. The flashlight up above disintegrated, and a man screamed. Then, little scarlet points of fire began to lance downward from the landing, to the accompaniment of the trip-hammer tapping of a machine-gun. Lead hammered into the stairs.

But Steve was not there. Instead of going up or down by the stairs, he had vaulted the bannister—with agility. He landed on his feet on the carpeted hall of the first floor, facing that opening door. It was open about six inches, and the muzzle of a sub-machine gun was coming out.

Steve didn't give it a chance to open any farther. He sent four shots from his left-hand gun crashing in quick succession into that aperture. The door sagged open, and the gun-muzzle dropped to the floor.

Stephen Klaw raced across the hall and kicked the door wide open. He sprang inside, with his guns going first. But there was nothing to shoot at in here. The apartment was empty, unfurnished. The dead machine-gunner lay just inside the door, on top of his gun.

Steve shoved him over, and picked up the tommy-gun.

The hallway was still thundering with gunfire. The gunner on the next landing was firing burst after burst down the stairs.

Steve waited.

At last the man above stopped. He called out cautiously, "Hey, Joe! Did we get him—"

Stephen Klaw didn't give that man a chance to finish. He stepped out quickly and raised the machine-gun and depressed the trip. The weapon bucked in his hands. Flame stabbed upward, cutting the man's words off in his throat, transforming them into a scream.

Stephen Klaw stopped after the first burst. A machine-gun came bouncing down the stairs. It was followed by a body. The body rolled over and over, and ended up at the foot of the stairs.

The stench of cordite was high in Stephen's nostrils, and the echo of the gunfire was in his ears. It was reverberating through the whole building.

He heard some one groan up above, and then he heard footsteps retreating upward.

He felt around in the clothes of the dead machine-gunner at his feet, and found what he sought—a flashlight.

He flicked it on. The man who had rolled down the stairs was dead, his chest virtually shot away by that single burst.

Steve raced up the stairs to the next landing. Here lay the body of the man with the flashlight, whom he had shot first. He was on his face. Steve turned him over, beamed the light into his face. He sucked in his breath.

It was Pete Sardis. Two of Steve's slugs, barely six inches apart, had caught him over the heart....

BUT THE thing that held Stephen Klaw's attention was the fact that Pete Sardis was bound and gagged. His hands were tied behind him. There was a dirty handkerchief stuffed in his mouth and held there by a strap around his head. And the shattered flashlight was tied to Sardis' arm by a strip of wire.

They had used Sardis as bait all right. They had bound and gagged him, and stuck the flashlight on him, and dragged him here to be shot by the first slugs from Steve's gun. Then they had figured to shoot down Stephen Klaw, and untie Sardis.

The evidence would be there for everyone to see—the G-man had been killed while attempting to capture Pete Sardis. It would have been just another kind of accident, with no back-trail to Mr. Zero to justify an F.B.I. investigation. Mr. Zero had freed Sardis from the threat of hanging, had no doubt collected the hundred and fifty thousand dollars from him, and then had deliberately sacrificed him.

In Stephen Klaw's ears there still sounded the patter of retreating footsteps limping upstairs. One of these gunmen was getting away. And from the sounds, the man must be wounded.

Steve raced up the stairs after the man. Several doors opened tentatively, then closed again swiftly as the house-holders realized that the shooting was not over yet.

The man above was moving slowly, and Steve caught him before he reached the top floor. The man turned, snarling, as Steve's flashlight pinned him to the stairs, and raised a tommy-gun weakly. But he had not the strength to hold it. It fell from his hands.

"Oh, Gawd, don't shoot!" he called out weakly—and fainted.

Steve came up quickly and examined him. The man was hit in the shoulder and in the groin. Steve seized his arm, slung him across his back none too gently, and carried him downstairs.

He emerged into the street to hear a siren clamoring in the distance. The girl was still handcuffed to the wheel of the coupé in front of the door. The limousine down at the corner roared into life and came racing down toward him. One of the doors came open.

"Git in, quick!" some one shouted.

This was the getaway car—intended for any of the gunmen who might survive the battle with Stephen Klaw.

Steve's eyes glittered. He held the unconscious gunman over his right shoulder. He had an automatic in his left hand. He raised the automatic and fired three times at the limousine—once at the driver, and twice at the man who was holding the door open in the back. Guns roared....

Some one in the car screamed. The scream ended in a gurgle. The driver slumped over the wheel. His foot must have pressed down on the accelerator, because the limousine didn't stop, but kept on going right past the house, gaining speed and swerving crazily.

It struck a fire hydrant across the street and virtually stood up on its front wheels, then went over the hydrant and hit a building with a sickening crash.

STEPHEN KLAW carried the gunman to the coupé without once looking at the wrecked limousine. He dumped the unconscious man into the seat, pushed him over close to the girl, then crowded in beside the inert figure.

The girl was looking at him with wide eyes. She wore a trembling smile—almost of gladness—on her lips. "You—you're alive—and unhurt!"

He nodded grimly. "Thanks to your warning." He reached over and unlocked the handcuffs. "Think you can drive?"

"Yes, yes."

"Then let's go. That siren is getting louder. And people are looking out of their windows."

The girl reached down and turned on the ignition, and got the coupé going. It was cramped driving with the wounded and bleeding gunman slumping against her.

Stephen Klaw, looking at her sideways, saw that her teeth were pressing into her lower lip. She turned the corner just as a police car screamed into the street at the other end. She drove swiftly for several blocks, making two or three turns. At last she slowed up.

"Where do you want to go?" she asked.

He shrugged. "I guess there isn't a safe place in Falcon City for you after tonight," he said. "Mr. Zero will be after you for helping me get away."

"I don't care for myself!" she exclaimed. "It's my brother. It's what'll happen to George."

"What's your first name?" he asked her. "Mary?"

"No. Nina. Nina Payne."

"All right, Nina. Stick with me," he said. "Gamble your brother's life on this deal. I'm not playing a lone hand here in Falcon City. There are two more men here—two of the best. They're working somewhere. We have a good chance of winning now. If we win, I'll take care of your brother. If Zero wins, your brother loses out. It's a fifty-fifty gamble. Will you take it and play along with me all the way?"

She kept on driving slowly for five minutes, staring straight ahead into the night. Suddenly she squared her chin and spoke. "I'll do it! I'd trust you with my own life—gladly. If George knew you, I'm sure he'd gamble on you. I'll do it!"

"Good girl!" he said quietly. He reached across the unconscious gunman and pressed her hand, on the wheel.

"Now—where can we take this bozo—where Zero can't get him back?"

"There's one place where he'd never think to look for him—my apartment." she said. "Zero doesn't know yet that I've double-crossed him. No one is alive back there to tell him."

"All right," said Stephen Klaw. "Your apartment."

CHAPTER 6
DEATH LIES IN WAIT

S HE LIVED in a corner building in one of the quieter residential sections, on the third floor of a self-service elevator apartment. She parked around the corner, in front of the service elevator. She kept control of herself like a real thoroughbred while Stephen Klaw lifted up the wounded gunman and carried him on his shoulder in through the basement to the service elevator. She operated the elevator.

Steve carried the man into the small two-room apartment, and put him on the bed. He went through the man's pockets, and found papers which identified him as Joseph Lukas, of Chicago. He set to work to cleanse the two wounds, with Nina helping him by bringing hot water and bandages.

While he was working, the man opened his eyes and groaned.

Steve said tonelessly, "Well, Lukas, you're at the end of the trail."

"I'm going to die?"

"No," the G-man said. "You're shot twice but it's nothing that a doctor can't fix up. How about Mr. Zero? Who is he?"

"Go to hell!" snarled Lukas.

Steve's slate-gray eyes remained expressionless. "Okay, Lukas!" He put down the bandage and turned and started out of the room.

"When—when is the doctor coming?" asked the thug.

Steve turned at the door. "Doctor—Hell! I'm going to let you bleed to death."

39

"Gawd! No! You can't do that. You're a G-man. G-men don't let guys bleed to death!"

"*This* G-man does!" said Steve. He went out and shut the door, cutting off Joe Lukas' frantic voice.

Nina Payne was standing in the living-room, with face flushed, and hands at her breast. Her eyes questioned him terribly. "Steve! You can't let him die!"

"You want to save your brother, don't you?"

She dropped her eyes. "It—it's too cruel!"

"Did Zero or his men have mercy on you? On your brother?" he asked. "This is war. It must be fought like war. We must kill or be killed. Lukas will weaken."

He took her by the arm. "If you are Mr. Zero's contact man, you must have some way of getting in touch with him in an emergency."

She nodded.

"How?"

She told him, "I call a private, unlisted number—Falcon Seven-two-one-two-one. It never answers. But he must have some way of hearing it ring. He always calls back within an hour or two." She hurried on as she caught the gleam of interest in Steve's eyes. "Oh, it's no good trying to trace him through that number. I—I tried it. It's a private line, and the phone company won't disclose the name of the subscriber. But I have a friend in the central office, and I got it. The number is under the name of a Mr. John Jones. It's a small office, in the Strand Building, in City Hall Square, right behind the county courthouse. No one ever comes near it. I—I've watched it for hours. I—"

She was interrupted by the ringing of the telephone.

They looked at each other silently. Her eyes were wide with consternation. She whispered, *"Mr. Zero!"* Woodenly, she picked up the phone and said, "Yes?"

A voice crackled over the wire, and her eyes flashed. She shook her head in the negative, to indicate to Steve that it wasn't Mr. Zero.

The voice rattled on excitedly for a full minute. Steve could see growing excitement in her face, and in the swift rising and falling of her breasts as she listened.

The voice stopped, and she said, "Wait a minute, Runcie."

She covered the phone with her hand and whispered excitedly to Steve, "It's Phil Runcie. He's a doctor who has a private sanitarium out on Glendale Road. He does a lot of work for Mr. Zero. I think he has something to do with the hold that this Zero has over Judge Harley."

"Yes?"

"Runcie is in trouble," she explained. "He says two terrible men attacked his place and have taken it over. He just barely escaped. I don't like the way he sounds. There seems to be something the matter with him now."

"What does he want you to do?" Steve asked.

"He wants to tell Mr. Zero. Zero controls the police force. He could send a crew of police out there to recapture the place and kill those men."

Steve smiled. "I think I know who those two terrible men are." He pressed her arm tightly. "Tell Runcie to come here. Tell him one of Zero's men is wounded and needs treatment."

SHE GASPED, but obeyed. She spoke quickly into the phone. Runcie's quavering voice objected. She insisted. He began to talk very loud to drown her out, so that Steve could hear what he was saying. His words were jumbled, however.

Nina covered the phone once more.

"I think there's some one with him," she said. "Some one who's forcing him to make the call."

"I don't doubt it," said Steve. "Tell him to come here, no matter what the situation is—that you'll take care of it."

She repeated that into the phone. Then, at Runcie's acquiescence, she hung up.

"Put in that call for Mr. Zero," Steve ordered her. "When he calls back, tell him what Runcie told you."

Her eyes widened, but she did as he directed. She called Falcon 72121. There was no answer. She left the receiver off the hook, so it would continue to ring.

Steve nodded, and went into the bedroom.

Joe Lukas was bleeding like a stuck pig.

He had been calling out feebly to Steve all the time that they were in the next room, but Steve hadn't heeded.

"For Gawd's sake," Lukas begged, "get a doctor. Those slugs are burning me up!"

Steve came over and stood grinning down at him mercilessly. "You know who I am?"

"Yeah."

"You've heard of me?" Steve asked.

"Yeah. You—you're a killer. I—I should of known better than to take the job!" Lukas groaned.

"Then you ought to know I'll let you die if you don't talk."

"Gawd, there's nothin' I can talk about. I don't know who Mr. Zero is. We get our orders on the phone!" Lukas winced.

"Too bad, Lukas. Too bad you have to die."

"Wait! There—there's one thing I can talk about," the man said. "It—it'll land me in the death house. It's murder. But—Gawd how those slugs hurt! Maybe I can beat that rap. I—I can't beat this rap—without a doctor."

"All right, talk," Steve said. "If it's worth it, I'll get you a doctor."

"It—it's murder. I—I killed the man that that guy George Payne was framed for."

Stephen Klaw turned just in time to steady Nina Payne, who was suddenly swaying on her feet. She clenched her hands and forced her swaying body upright.

"Go—*on!*" she whispered.

Stephen Klaw took out paper and a fountain-pen. "Talk!" he ordered. "I'll write it—and you'll sign it!"

Joe Lukas talked. He exonerated George Payne. He told how he had been ordered to kill a man—ordered by the sharp, metallic voice of Mr. Zero. He told how he had left a key ring of George Payne's at the scene of the murder—the key ring that had convicted Nina's brother.

When Steve finished waiting, Lukas scrawled his signature. Steve and Nina witnessed it.

"All right," said Steve. "Lie quietly. A doctor will be here right away. Take it easy."

Nina went into the next room and hung up the receiver.

Almost as soon as she did so, the phone rang. She grew suddenly tense, and picked up the receiver. "Yes?"

A sharp, metallic voice came over the wire. "You wanted me?"

"Yes." She looked inquiringly at Steve, and when he nodded, she hurried on. "Doctor Runcie's sanitarium has been attacked by two men. Runcie thinks they are G-men. He said to tell you that they have taken over the place. He says you will know how important it is."

For what seemed an infinite period of time there was silence on the wire. Then the metallic voice spoke again. "All right. Remain at your phone. I will call you again."

"What do you want Runcie to do? I told him to come here."

"Let him wait there." Mr. Zero hung up.

"Good," said Steve. "I hope Johnny and Dan had sense enough to clear out of there with whatever they found."

"Runcie ought to be here any minute," she said. "He was phoning from the city."

The doorbell rang.

Stephen Klaw took out one of his automatics. "Open it," he said.

She went to the door and pulled it open.

Doctor Runcie, fat and sweating, with a bleeding lip, was standing there. He started to say something, but someone shoved him hard from behind and sent him sprawling into the room.

Dan Murdoch and Johnny Kerrigan, shoulder to shoulder, pushed in through the doorway, with guns in their fists.

"Everybody hold it!" Murdoch barked. "This is the law—" He broke off when he saw Stephen Klaw.

"Hell, Johnny," he said. "The Shrimp beat us to it!"

Murdoch and Kerrigan came into the room grinning, and put their guns away.

"Hyah, Shrimp?" said Kerrigan.

"Hello, Mopes," said Steve.

"Glad to see you alive," said Murdoch.

"Nuts to you," said Stephen Klaw.

That was all. But the glow in the eyes of Johnny Kerrigan, and the faint twitch of the thin lips of Dan Murdoch, showed more than words the relief they felt at seeing Stephen Klaw still alive and kicking.

AFTER MURDOCH and Kerrigan, an assorted group of people entered the small room. Judge Harley came in, still holding a gun on the big burly man in white. Then came Emma Harley, supporting her daughter. There was also a boy of thirteen, who turned but to be the son of the chairman of the state parole board. He had also been released from the sanitarium. And his presence explained why so many gangsters had been prematurely paroled in the past six months.

Steve Klaw took Runcie by the collar and bundled him into the bedroom.

"Do the best you can for him, Runcie. We need him. Let him die, and I'll kick your face in!"

He came back into the living-room. Nina Payne was brewing tea for the women. Kerrigan was trying to get a little attention from Nina, and Murdoch was fiddling with the radio, looking for shortwave.

Kerrigan swiftly told Steve what they had done at the sanitarium. "I brought Runcie back there after he told me about this phone number. We bundled everybody in two cars and headed back for the city. Then we made Runcie call this number, figuring it would give us a lead to Mr. Zero's contact man. Imagine our surprise when she told Runcie to come over, and gave him the address!"

Murdoch got the radio set for police calls, and came over.

"So it adds up to this: Zero's hold on the superior court is broken. Judge Harley doesn't have to take Zero's orders any more, now that he has his daughter back. But everything else remains intact for Zero. He still controls the police."

The radio sputtered to lift on the shortwave band, with a police announcer's voice:

"Attention all cars! Signal Forty-three! Block all exits from city. Stephen Klaw and two accomplices are wanted for murder. Stop all vehicles leaving town. Search carefully. Shoot to kill. These men are dangerous. Relay orders to patrolmen at all railroad and bus stations to watch for these men. They must not leave the city. All reserve patrolmen and all officers now off duty who hear this call are ordered to report to their precinct houses immediately for emergency duty in forming cordon around the city. I will repeat: *Shoot to kill...*"

"We'll fix that!" Steve said. He picked up the phone and put through a person-to-person call for the Director of the F.B.I.

at his home in Washington. In five minutes he was reporting to his chief.

"It means, sir," he finished, "that we still don't know who Mr. Zero is. But we have enough evidence of criminal conspiracy to violate the federal anti-racketeering law—enough to warrant our coming in strong. I suggest that you route as many agents as are available in near-by cities and order them to fly to Falcon City at once. There will be trouble popping any minute, and a show of force may be necessary."

"*Now!*" he said when he hung up. "Mr. Zero is looking for Kerrigan and Murdoch and Klaw—so Kerrigan and Murdoch and Klaw will go out and accommodate Mr. Zero!" He took Nina Payne aside. "Where did you say this office was in the name of John Jones, where Zero gets the phone calls he doesn't answer?"

"At the Strand Building," she told him. "Room Three-fifteen. The building is directly opposite the county courthouse."

"All right. When Zero calls you back, don't tell him that Judge Harley and these others are here. But tell him that I was here—and that I've gone to investigate a lead at the Strand Building."

Her eyes widened. "You—you're going to wait for him to get you?"

"We're going to wait for him to *try* to get us!" he corrected her. "We'll give him one last chance!"

As the three members of the F.B.I. Suicide Squad filed out of that room, Stephen Klaw saw Nina Payne looking after him as if she wanted to call him back.

He smiled, and closed the door.

CHAPTER 7
F.B.I. FINISH FIGHT

KERRIGAN AND Murdoch and Klaw braked their car to a stop directly before the entrance of the Strand Building. Across City Hall Park there was the wide facade of the county courthouse. At the north end of the park there was the low squat police headquarters building, where there seemed to be a lot of activity.

Murdoch grinned. "Those boys would eat nails if they knew we were right here watching them while they're blockading all the roads to cut us off!"

"Let's tell 'em," said Johnny Kerrigan.

"Nuts!" said Steve Klaw. "Let's go. We have work to do."

Kerrigan and Klaw got out of the car, leaving Murdoch on watch. They went up to the third floor, and tried the door of Room 315. It was locked.

Johnny tried to pick the lock, but couldn't make it. "It's some new-fangled contraption," he said. "I'll try the old shoulder-and-arm system."

He stepped back five feet, got set, and sent himself hurtling into the door. It splintered under the powerful impact of his heavy stevedore's shoulders, and he went sprawling inside.

Steve Klaw covered him with a gun, in case there was anyone lying in wait in the office. But there was nobody here now.

There was virtually no furniture in the little eight-by-ten room. There was a small ten-dollar desk, but no chair. There was a telephone on the desk. In one corner, near the window,

48

was the telephone box. Hooked to the wall alongside it there was another box. A wire led from this box out of the window.

Steve's eyes narrowed. He opened the window and looked out. Alongside it, screwed into the window frame, there was a contraption that looked like the blinkers on a dray-horse. Steve leaned far out to see what was between the blinkers. He heard Murdoch yelling from downstairs.

"Look out, Shrimp! I'd hate to have to catch you!"

But he didn't answer, because he had just made a discovery. There was a bulb of some sort between those blinkers.

He yelled down to Murdoch, "Walk across the park and see if a light goes on!"

Then he ducked in and said to Johnny Kerrigan, "I think I got something!"

He knelt on the floor and fiddled with the telephone box till he got the cover off. Then he shorted it so the bell jangled. He kept it ringing for a minute, then popped up and looked out of the window.

He could see Murdoch in the park. Dan was shaking his head in the negative. He motioned that he would go farther back.

Steve pointed to the county courthouse, and Murdoch nodded. He turned and trotted toward the courthouse building.

Johnny Kerrigan was scratching his head. "What's biting you, Shrimp?"

"This is how Zero gets notice that he's being called on this phone. When it rings, a light of some sort goes on outside. He sees it, and knows this phone is ringing. He doesn't have to come near this office. Apparently the light can only be seen from a certain spot, because of the blinkers. If we find that spot, we got a good chance of finding Mr. Zero."

"I hope," said Johnny, "that we find Mr. Zero before Mr. Zero finds us."

Steve had kept on short-circuiting the telephone box while they talked, causing the bell to ring constantly. Now he stopped, and looked out of the window. He couldn't see Murdoch, so he went back and rang it some more. He kept that up for five minutes, then looked out again.

There was still no sign of Murdoch, but suddenly the phone on the desk rang by itself.

Steve scooped it up.

"Shrimp!" It was Murdoch's voice "I'm in the county courthouse. I'm in the only office you can see that light from. Guess whose office?" He didn't give Steve a chance to guess. "No less a personage than the Honorable Grover Ellis—district attorney of Falcon County!"

"Boy!" said Steve. "He was the baby who offered to help me out! Come on back, Dan. The show ought to be starting any minute!"

He hung up and looked at Johnny Kerrigan. Johnny had heard what Murdoch said over the phone.

"Well, that breaks the case!"

"All we have to do is get out of here alive, Johnny—"

The telephone rang once more, and interrupted him.

This time it was Nina Payne. She was excited, and talking fast. "Steve! Mr. Zero called me just a few minutes ago. I told him you had gone to the Strand Building. He hung up at once. And just now there are new orders going out over the short-wave. All cars are ordered to surround the Strand Building. All the reserves are being ordered there, with machine-guns and tear-gas—"

"Okay, Nina. I see them. They're coming across from police headquarters. Listen, if we don't get out of this—tell our chief that *Mr. Zero is Grover Ellis!*"

She cried out in anguish. "Steve! I Oh, God, don't let him die—"

STEPHEN KLAW hung up on her. He joined Johnny Kerrigan at the window. They saw Dan Murdoch in the park. He had been coming across, but he was cut off from them now, by a stream of blue-coated men who were running from the direction of police headquarters. Half a dozen squad cars were already at the curb, and men with riot guns were leaping out.

Steve said tightly, "Cover me, Johnny. I'm going down to cover the door. Got to keep them out of the building...."

He was out of the office before he finished, and as he almost tumbled down the stairs he already heard Kerrigan's heavy service revolver barking. Kerrigan was probably firing directly down, keeping the front entrance under fire so that the bluecoats couldn't enter.

Steve reached the lobby and took up a position behind the elevator shaft. He saw a group of bluecoats with tear-gas guns and riot guns, in a huddle well away from the angle of Johnny Kerrigan's fire. He could hear rifles popping out in the street. Men were firing up at Johnny.

They were not bona fide police but hired thugs, in cop uniforms—in the pay of Mr. Zero.

Grimly, Steve went into action. He leveled his two automatics, and let go with both of them into that huddled group.

Men fell under the twin hail of lead, and the group disintegrated. He saved three shots in one of his automatics, while he inserted a fresh clip in the other. By the time he had that done, Johnny Kerrigan had joined him behind the elevator shaft.

The police were approaching warily now, in open formation. Three men with tear-gas grenades were in the lead.

Johnny Kerrigan fired three times, and the three grenade throwers fell before they were within hurling distance of the door.

"Got to make them keep their distance," Johnny muttered: "I hate the smell of tear-gas."

"Me, too," said Steve.

"How many rounds you got, Shrimp?" Johnny asked.

"Two clips for each gun," Steve told him.

"Me, I got thirty cartridges. Not much between us."

"Well, I'm glad Murdoch is out of this," said Steve. "One of us ought to go back and say hello to the chief."

The police were employing new tactics. They were driving a squad car up on the sidewalk, with the evident intention of riding it directly through the door and into the lobby. The car was full of men, and as the car rolled to the door, they kept up a continuous fire.

"Well, it looks like curtains," said Johnny.

"So long, Shrimp, see you in Hell."

"So bug, Mope," said Steve. "See you in Hell."

And then the deadly work began. The car crashed through

the doorway, and a fusillade of lead swept the lobby, driving Johnny and Steve back behind the shaft. Steve dropped to the floor, poked a hand and an eye around the shaft, and snapped just one shot at the car. It splintered the windshield, pierced it, and hit the driver squarely in the forehead. The car stopped.

"That was a lucky shot," said Steve. "Let's go."

He and Johnny came out shooting, and the bluecoats, apparently never very enthusiastic about the whole thing, retreated, leaving the car in the doorway.

"Look," said Johnny. "Santa Claus!"

He jumped into the car and threw out the body of the dead driver. He got behind the wheel, and Steve climbed on the running-board and started to shoot at the police in the street, while Johnny backed the car out at top speed.

He swung out into the middle of the street, and lead came flying at them from every direction. Steve ducked inside the car.

"Let 'er go!"

Kerrigan put her in first and gave her plenty of gas. They sped down the street.

Across in the park, a squad car with a sub-machine gun rigged on the roof swung to rake them. Steve could see the gunner squinting in the sights.

"He'll get us, Johnny. It was a good try—"

He broke off, and began to curse softly under his breath.

"Look at that crazy devil!"

Dan Murdoch had run out in the street and had picked up a sub-machine gun from one of the fallen men.

And now, surrounded on every side by the enemy, exposed

to their fire, without protection of any kind, he was standing there spraddle-legged with the typewriter hugged against his shoulder, and he was spraying the machine-gunner on top of that truck!

He was deliberately throwing away his life to give Kerrigan and Klaw a chance!

MURDOCH LET go two bursts, and sent the gunner flying off his perch, before they got him. He staggered, with a ball in his back, and a tight, wild grin on his face. Then he deliberately turned around and sent a final burst in the direction from which the shot had come which felled him.

And then he sank to the ground.

A dozen police started to run toward his prone body.

"Johnny!" yelled Steve.

Johnny Kerrigan didn't need to be told twice. There was moisture in his eyes as he swung that car around in a crazy loop and sent it hurtling toward the group advancing on Dan Murdoch's prone body.

"Damn them!" he choked. "They shot him in the back!"

Steve Klaw was out on the running-board again, and emptying his last two clips at the group of bluecoats. They scattered, as much because of the rolling juggernaut of death which Kerrigan was hurtling at them, as because of Steve's shots.

Johnny stood on the brakes as they came abreast of Murdoch's body. He lifted his revolver and kept it spitting to cover Steve Klaw.

Steve leaped out, seized Murdoch's body, and dragged him into the car. At once, Johnny sent it flying ahead again.

Now the police began to concentrate lead upon them. If they could only get out of the square, they might have a chance. But—no. The street at the other end was blockaded by a row of cars. They'd have to crash these cars, or stop. Death was the end, either way....

Dan Murdoch was still gripping the machine-gun. Steve pried it loose from his fingers.

"Stop, Johnny. This is a good place to die."

Johnny braked the car. Steve swung out to face the mass of attackers, with a grim hard smile on his lips.

And then he involuntarily raised his eyes to the sky, attracted by the sudden upsurge of a new sound—the deadly drone of a diving airplane!

"Johnny!" he shouted. "It's an F.B.I. plane!"

The fighting ship was coming down at two hundred miles an hour in a terrific power-dive. The F.B.I. markings on its wings were plainly visible now, and the twin streams of tracer bullets from its synchronized machine-guns swept across the square just over the heads of the fleeing, panic-stricken blue-coats who were fighting to get out of that square. Those men, imported thugs from every slum section of the world, had no guts for this kind of fighting.

The F.B.I. plane had come out of its dive, and it was rising again, while a second and third plane wheeled overhead, prepared to dive if that warning was not heeded.

Now the first plane banked into the wind and came down on the broad plaza of City Hall Square. The director of the F.B.I. himself, climbed out of the cockpit.

Johnny Kerrigan started to run toward it, with Steve following him. But just then Steve caught a slither of movement near the edge of the square. He swung around and recognized the figure of the big man who had started to run.

"Stop!" he shouted. "Stop or I shoot!"

Grover Ellis swung toward him, snarling. He raised a long-barrelled revolver.

Stephen Klaw was still holding that sub-machine gun. That familiar glint came into his eyes. He leveled it and pulled the trip.

Slugs marched back and forth across the body of Grover Ellis. Not till the man was riddled like a sieve did Stephen Klaw let up on the trip. Then he threw the gun from him and climbed into the car where Dan Murdoch lay.

"I paid off for you, Dan," he started to say. And then he saw Murdoch's eyes flicker. "Dan!" he yelled.

Murdoch's face was pale. There was blood under his shoulders. He stirred, and opened his eyes weakly. "Hyah, Shrimp?" he murmured.

"Hyah, Mope," said Stephen Klaw. "Glad to see you alive."

As the director approached with Johnny Kerrigan, Stephen Klaw turned and faced him, with a very suspicious trace of moisture in his eyes. He gulped.

"Glad to report, sir," he said, "that there are no casualties in the Suicide Squad today!"

THE SUICIDE SQUAD
REPORTS FOR DEATH

CHAPTER 1
BLOOD MONEY FOR G-MEN

JOHNNY KERRIGAN was not as drunk as he looked. Russ Kimber had bought him a lot of drinks. Johnny didn't seem to notice that the bartender was filling Kimber's glass nine-tenths with water, Johnny's was nine-tenths Scotch. But what Russ Kimber didn't know was that when Johnny Kerrigan really set his mind to it, he could handle more liquor than any man living—with the possible exception of Stephen Klaw and Dan Murdoch, his two sidekicks on the F.B.I. Suicide Squad.

Russ Kimber's small, fox-like eyes bored into Kerrigan's. His still lips were twisted into an abortive attempt at a friendly smile.

"So you're not here officially as a G-man, Johnny?"

Johnny Kerrigan blinked at him owlishly. "Jus' as a private citizen, Kimber ol' boy. My friend Frank Robbins told me you eloped with his kid daughter, Selma. Now she found out what kind of guy you are, she wants to go home, but you won't let her. So I'm here to sort of convince you."

Kimber's little eyes were sharper than ever. "Take a tip from me, Kerrigan. Forget about the whole thing. Believe me, there's too much involved for me to give Selma up."

"Sure, sure, I know," Johnny said. "You figure to get Frank

57

58

Robbins knocked off, so Selma will inherit the estate. Then you'll take it from her."

The other stared.

Johnny Kerrigan shook his head ponderously. " 'Tisn' right, Kimber. I'm making you a friendly prop—proposition—let Selma come home with me. And give her a divorce."

A shrewd gleam came into Russ Kimber's eyes. He moved closer along the bar, and dropped his voice. "You don't make much salary with the F.B.I., Johnny. How can you live on the salary they pay you?"

Johnny seemed to think that over for a little while. Then he nodded ponderously. " 'Swhat I always ask myself, Kimber ol' boy. How can I live on my salary?"

"Would you like to make some real dough?"

"How much real dough?"

"Say, ten grand."

Johnny grinned fatuously. "What must I do?"

"Nothing much. Just walk out of here and go home," Kimber said. "You can tell Frank Robbins that he hasn't got a leg to stand on. I didn't violate any law when I married Selma. Tell him it's okay, and you make ten grand!"

"Nix," said Johnny Kerrigan. "I came here to find Selma and take her home. Won't go without her. I'll take this joint apart to find her."

Russ Kimber scowled. "Don't be a sap, Kerrigan. She's not here. I sent her away."

"Then—" Johnny grinned with the shrewdness of the true drunk—"why you wanna pay me ten grand to go away?"

"Because we don't want trouble with you," Kimber said. "You got a reputation. The boss doesn't want to tangle with you—if possible."

"What boss?"

"My boss."

"Who's your boss?" and now Johnny's eyes narrowed.

KIMBER HESITATED. He looked around the room. Kimber's Bar and Grill was well-filled tonight. There were thirty or forty people at the bar and tables, mostly men. Kimber exchanged glances with several of them. These were his plug-uglies, toughs he could rely on to see to it that Johnny Kerrigan never left this place alive if he learned too much. There were only two men whom Kimber didn't know. They were sitting at a corner table, drinking beer. One was dark-haired and dark-eyed, slim and handsome. The other was smaller, wiry-looking, but hardly more than a kid—or so Kimber thought. If anything started, those two would have to be taken care of, too—so there'd be no witness to tell what had happened to the big drunken G-man.

Kimber grinned thinly, and turned back to Johnny. "You've heard of—the 'General?'"

Johnny Kerrigan whistled. "So you work for the General?"

"Yes. Now you know. The General offers you ten grand to step out of the picture right now. Lay off. Go home. It'll be healthier for you—and more profitable."

Johnny Kerrigan peered bleary-eyed at Kimber. "Ten grand is a lot of dough. That girl—Selma Robbins—must be here. Otherwise you wouldn't offer me all that dough."

"Okay," Kimber snarled. "Have it your way. Selma is here. She's upstairs, guarded by machine-guns. Neither you nor the whole F.B.I. could get to her. Now, do you take the ten grand and lay off? Or do we have to get tough with you?"

Suddenly Johnny Kerrigan started to laugh. He put out one huge paw and wrapped his fingers around Russ Kimber's neck.

"Get tough!" he said.

Kimber's face grew red as the circulation of blood was choked off by that terrible grip. He pawed at his shoulder holster and dragged out an automatic.

Johnny Kerrigan laughed again, and took Kimber's wrist in his left hand and bent it backward. Kimber's lips whitened with the new pain, and he let the automatic fall to the floor.

"Now," said Johnny, "you and I are going upstairs and find Selma Robbins!"

He pushed away from the bar, holding Kimber in the air effortlessly by the back of his neck. But he had not taken two steps when the attack came. Half a dozen of the thugs seated at the nearest tables sprang to their feet and began to close in on him.

Johnny Kerrigan didn't even look at them. He just kept moving toward the rear.

One of the thugs reached over to the bar and picked up a half-full whiskey bottle. He raised it by the neck, started to bring it down in a smashing blow to Johnny's face. Johnny Kerrigan didn't try to duck the blow. He just kept going.

Somewhere in the room an automatic barked once. The thug remained standing with his hand in the air. The whiskey bottle slid from his grip. An expression of intense surprise was stamped on his face. Then blood spurted from a small hole in the center of his forehead, and he toppled right at Johnny Kerrigan's feet.

The other gunmen turned around, startled.

The two men who had been sitting in the corner had kicked back their chairs and jumped on top of the table. It was the smaller of the two who had fired the single shot. He had two automatics, one in each hand. He was grinning wickedly, and there was a hard gleam in his slate-gray eyes.

"Everybody please stand still!" he said.

Johnny Kerrigan laughed his deep, booming laugh. "Not bad, Steve. I couldn't have shot straighter myself!"

He stepped over the dead thug, still carrying Kimber by the scruff of the neck. He straight-armed one of the astounded gunmen in his path, and made for the rear.

The bartender came up from behind the bar with a wide-mouthed .45, which he pointed at Johnny.

Steve Klaw, still grinning, fired once more. The bartender went crashing backward against his bottles, with a slug in his chest.

That seemed to be the signal for the paralyzed gunmen to swing into action. Guns flashed, feet slithered along the floor, as they spread out to take these impudent intruders.

And for the first time the tall, dark-haired man beside Steve Klaw spoke…. "Shoot me first, you lugs!" he drawled.

They stopped, struck dumb with the terror at sight of the thing he was holding up in the air.

It was a small hand grenade.

He had already drawn the pin. The only thing that kept the detonator from striking was his finger on the safety lever on the side of the grenade.

Dan Murdoch smiled very engagingly at the pallid crowd of thugs, and flipped the pin out among them.

"Observe," he said in his soft-spoken manner, "that if I should be shot, I would naturally drop the grenade. When I drop it, the lever is released. When the lever is released, the grenade goes—*plop*. And so does everybody in this room. Also, if you try to shoot either Steve Klaw or Johnny Kerrigan, I will certainly throw this little toy out among you. We'll all go to hell together!"

There was grim silence in the room for a second. Then a voice said sneeringly, "He'll never do it—"

Another voice, inspired by awe, broke in.

"He will! He will! That's Murdoch. And the little one is Killer Klaw. My Gawd, the whole damned Suicide Squad is here!"

"That's right," said Stephen Klaw. "The Suicide Squad. We're getting the Robbins girl. Who wants to stop us?"

At least a dozen of the gunmen had their weapons out. But nobody raised a gun. The reputation of the F.B.I. Suicide Squad was too terrible to be trifled with by these guttersnipes.

EVERYBODY IN the underworld had heard of them— Kerrigan and Murdoch and Klaw. The three Black Sheep of the F.B.I.—three men who were never sent on a regular routine assignment, but who always rated the calls where death was almost a certainty. Not so long ago there had been five of them. Now there were only three. Tomorrow there might be only two—or one—or none. But one thing was sure—those three devils wouldn't die easy. They weren't easy to kill. They'd take plenty of men to Hell with them when they died. And the gangsters in *Kimber's Bar & Grill* right now, didn't want to die.

So they stood still and tense while big Johnny Kerrigan moved his way across the room, and kicked open the door at the rear. He shook Russ Kimber like a rat, and set him on his feet.

"You first, pal!" He turned and waved to Murdoch and Klaw. "Keep the rats interested, boys. I'm going up." He gave Kimber a shove, sent him stumbling into the hallway. Then he snaked out his gun, followed him.

Almost at once, a door opened at the far end of the hall, and a man was framed there, with a sub-machine gun at his shoulder.

Kimber uttered a frightened squawk, and dropped to the floor. Johnny Kerrigan fired five times fast at the machine-gunner.

But the typewriter was already stuttering. It sent a hail of lead pouring into the hall. The slugs swept a little high, and by the time the gunner got his sights adjusted, blood was pouring from his body where Johnny's shots had hit him.

He stumbled forward, and a last burst escaped from the machine-gun. One shot nicked Johnny Kerrigan along the ribs, another caught him in the thigh. Then the rest of the hail swept down lower and riddled Russ Kimber, where he cowered on the floor.

Johnny Kerrigan was sent staggering sideways against the wall. He steadied his revolver against his elbow, and emptied it into the doorway, where a second man had appeared. This one dropped, and a third stepped into his place, also with a machine-gun. He raised it.

Johnny Kerrigan's gun was empty. He could not retreat, because of his injured leg. He could not charge, either. He shrugged.

"Okay, mug," he said. "I can take it!"

"Here it is, sucker!" said the machine-gunner, and reached for the trip....

CHAPTER 2
DEATH ON ORDER

OUT IN the barroom, Stephen Klaw and Dan Murdoch listened to the sounds of the battle in the hallway. Dan held the grenade high in the air, grinning affably at the tense and watchful gunmen, who were crowded together against the bar. Steve Klaw held his two automatics ready, in case any of them should get up courage enough to rush them.

They heard the first burst from the machine-gun, then the second. They heard Johnny Kerrigan say, *"Okay, mug, I can take it!"*

Steve Klaw's lips tightened. "I'm going after him, Dan!" he said, and leaped from the table.

He cleared the space in front of the cowering gunmen, and sprang through the doorway. He saw Johnny Kerrigan facing the machine-gun, saw the gunner ready to pull the trip.

Steve Klaw's two automatics began to roar in beautifully synchronized time. *One, two—one, two—one....*

The gunner never pulled the trip. He went hurtling backward, his arms flailing the air, the machine-gun dropping from nerveless fingers.

Steve Klaw jumped over the supine body of Russ Kimber. "Get out, Johnny," he shouted. "I'll get the Robbins girl for you!"

He raced down the hallway, and through the door. There was a steep flight of stairs here, and Steve took them two at a time, with his guns leading the way. Halfway up, he fired twice, to discourage anyone who might be waiting at the top.

Then he was on the landing. Nobody was there. He looked around, and saw Johnny Kerrigan painfully dragging himself up the stairs, one at a time. "Go back, Johnny," he called. "I can handle this."

"Nix," groaned Kerrigan. "Always—like to finish—what I start!" He kept coming up.

Steve Klaw shrugged. He started down the hall. There were doors on either side. He tried each in turn, flinging them open, peering inside. He looked in three rooms that way—found nothing. As he came to the fourth room, he heard a shuffling inside, and the quick sound of a scuffle. Then a girl's voice came clear and loud.

"Don't come in, Johnny. They're waiting for—" Her words were cut off suddenly.

Steve Klaw's eye glittered. He reached over, turned the knob and pushed the door open. As he did this, he stepped quickly to one side. At once a fusillade of shots burst through the open doorway. They spattered against the opposite wall, smashing away the plaster.

Steve Klaw dropped to his knees. At the far end of the hall he saw Johnny Kerrigan crawl up the top step, drag himself forward. He motioned to Kerrigan to lie still, then poked his gun and face around the edge of the open doorway from which the shots were still coming. He was close to the floor. He saw two men in the room. One was holding the girl, Selma Robbins, around the waist covering her mouth with his other hand. The second man was shooting steadily with two heavy revolvers at the doorway.

Steve Klaw got only a quick glimpse of the interior of the room. The man holding Selma Robbins saw him, yelled a warning to his partner. But he yelled too late.

Steve fired twice. He got the two-gun man high in the stomach. His second shot, fired more carefully, caught the other man full in the face—over Selma's shoulder.

Steve Klaw came lithely to his feet and sprang into the room just in time to catch Selma Robbins as she swayed.

"Hold everything, kid," Steve told her. "This is no time to faint!"

SELMA ROBBINS was a slim-waisted, chestnut-haired girl of nineteen or twenty. She stared at Steve, gulped. "You—you're not Johnny Kerrigan. I—I thought Johnny was coming for me."

"Johnny's here, all right. Come on. We have to get out of this!" He started to drag her toward the door—suddenly he stopped short.

The whole building was shaken by a tremendous concussion.

The floors shook. Plaster fell from the walls and ceiling. Window panes were shattered.

"Dan Murdoch!" Steve exclaimed. "Those rats must have tried to rush him and he threw the grenade!" He rushed out into the hall with Selma, almost fell over Johnny Kerrigan, who had crawled up to the door.

Flames were already roaring up the stairs at the far end of the hall. They could not get out that way.

"God!" groaned Johnny Kerrigan. "Dan'll burn to death—if he's not dead already!"

He pushed himself up to his feet. "I'm going down there and see what's left of him."

"Like hell you are!" said Steve Klaw. "You're shot up. You could never make it. Here, take one of my guns—and get Selma back in that room. You can go down the fire-escape with her."

He gave Johnny Kerrigan no chance to argue. He thrust the gun in his hand, dashed down the hall. When he got to the stairs, the flames were lancing up hungrily. He took off his coat, wrapped it around his head, and plunged down the stairs.

Kerrigan groaned. He swayed on his feet, and glared at Selma Robbins.

"Damn it," he said, "why did you have to get mixed up with Kimber? You've cost the lives of two of the best men living. You're not worth it!"

There were tears in her eyes. "I didn't know—"

Kerrigan gave her no chance to finish. "Come on," he said gruffly.

He led her back into the room where the two men lay whom

Steve had shot. He was swaying on his feet, and there was sweat on his face. Blood seeped through his coat on the right side, and also down his right trousers leg. But he held himself erect.

He knelt over one of the dead men, pulled back his coat. A small button was pinned to the man's vest. It was a cheap brass button, stamped out by machine. The stamped figure on the button represented a man in shirtsleeves, standing, and holding two swords, which were crossed over his breast. There was no lettering on the button.

Grimly, Johnny Kerrigan thrust the button into his pocket. Then he got painfully to his feet and motioned Selma Robbins to the window. He peered out past the fire-escape bars, and frowned.

The street below was filled with the gunmen who had been in the barroom with Dan Murdoch. They were thronging the sidewalk and the gutter, and some of them were looking up at the window.

As his head showed, they fired. Just in time, he ducked back. He looked blankly at Selma.

"I don't get it," he said. "I thought Dan Murdoch threw the grenade down there. I thought he killed all those rats—and himself as well. But they're out there—*alive!*"

He turned back to the window, and saw that a policeman had come running around the corner. The officer was tugging at his gun as he ran. But he got no chance to use it. A half-dozen shots took him full in the chest, and he went down.

Kerrigan snarled, and fired three times. Each shot was well-aimed, and three of the thugs fell. Johnny didn't know how many cartridges were left in the clip, but hoped there were at least a couple more.

"Get out on the fire-escape," he told Selma Robbins. "Climb down. I'll follow, and cover you. It's the only way out of this trap. The flames will reach us in about two minutes—and I doubt if the fire engines will get here in time."

Selma nodded wordlessly, and started for the window.

At that moment, a wide gun-barrel was suddenly thrust in at the window, and Johnny caught a glimpse of a man with a cap, leering at him. It was a tommy-gun. The man must have come down the fire-escape from an upper floor, to get him.

JOHNNY THRUST Selma Robbins away, and fired at the same time. He pulled the trigger again and again, but only one shot was left. That single bullet was enough, however. It took the machine-gunner directly between the eyes. He fell forward, and lay half in, half out of the window.

Johnny Kerrigan's eyes were gleaming. He reached over now, seized the tommy-gun.

"Go ahead, Selma," he said.

He pushed her toward the window, and, at the same time, turned the tommy-gun down toward the street. He pulled the trip. Lead sprayed from it among the gathered gunmen below. It cut through them like a scythe, and they scattered in panic, leaving a dozen of their number in the gutter.

Selma Robbins was out on the fire-escape now, and climbing down. Kerrigan followed her, keeping the gun trained on the street. A couple of desultory shots came his way, but they were too far away to do any damage. In a moment he and Selma Robbins had reached the street.

The whole building was in flames. Fire was pouring from the street entrance.

Johnny Kerrigan looked toward the doorway, somberly. Steve Klaw and Dan Murdoch were in there. He was filled with a terrible, murderous desire to avenge them.

He forgot about Selma Robbins, crouching against the wall. He saw only the figures of the scattered gunmen—watching him, like vultures, from a distance. He felt dizzy. His two wounds were throbbing, sending fiery messages of pain to his brain. Another man would have been unconscious by this time, but Johnny Kerrigan was holding to his feet by sheer brute, astounding strength.

He took a swaying step forward, aimed the machine-gun, and pulled the trip. He sprayed lead all the way down the street, and had the satisfaction of seeing two men fall before the rest of them could scamper to safety. The machine-gun drum was empty. He flung it from him, uttered a sobbing cry, and turned to go back into the flaming inferno of the building. He picked up a discarded gun that lay in the street—fired a final shot at a lingering thug.

Fire-engine bells clanged in the distance, and a police patrol siren screamed.

Johnny Kerrigan heard none of those. He was out on his feet. Only one thought persisted in the subconscious part of his mind—to go in there and die with Steve and Dan. He took two staggering steps forward, then stopped. His mouth opened.

For a ghastly, flaming figure came marching out of the burning doorway. It was Steve Klaw. He walked with difficulty, because he had Dan Murdoch over his shoulder. Both his and Murdoch's clothes were on fire, and Stephen Klaw's face was blistered, burned. But he *walked*, his gun still in his hand. He kept going until he got clear of the blaze. Then he keeled over, with the unconscious Dan Murdoch on top of him.

Johnny Kerrigan uttered a queer, choked cry, and sprang forward. He pulled off his own coat, began to beat out the fire in Steve's and Dan's clothing. He kept up those mechanical slapping motions long after there was actually any need for them.

It was thus that the fire engines and the police emergency cars found him. As soon as they took the coat from his numb fingers, he closed his eyes and collapsed.

Selma Robbins, sobbing softly, took his head in her lap and stroked his face. She watched them carry Steve Klaw and Dan Murdoch into the ambulance, then return for Johnny Kerrigan.

"They did it all for me!" she said—and fainted.

CHAPTER 3
THE ARMY OF DEATH

S UNLIGHT WAS streaming in through the hospital window, and splashing across three beds. Steve Klaw lay in the first bed, his face all swathed in bandages, like a mummy. Only a narrow slit enabled his eyes to peer out.

Dan Murdoch lay in the next bed smoking a cigarette, with one eye on the door, lest the nurse come in and catch him.

Johnny Kerrigan was sitting up in the last bed, with a newspaper which he was reading to them. It was a four-day old newspaper, but Murdoch and Klaw listened avidly to the lead story on page one.

SUICIDE SQUAD DOES IT AGAIN
FIVE KILLED, SEVEN WOUNDED BY KERRIGAN, MURDOCH AND KLAW IN SPECTACULAR GUN BATTLE

Last night, the three notorious desperadoes of the F.B.I. staged an attack upon a peaceable place of business, without benefit of a search warrant. The fact that all their victims were criminals with long records does not excuse the conduct of these notorious gunmen.

This paper has often wondered why these professional killers have not long ago been summarily dismissed from the Federal Bureau of Investigation. No doubt, their brilliant previous accomplishments have influenced the Director to keep then on the rolls. But the time has come....

Johnny Kerrigan stopped reading, groaned. "I dragged you two guys into this. It was a personal matter with me. And now we're all in Dutch. I can just imagine what the Director will have to say when he gets here."

Dan Murdoch grinned thinly. "Forget it, Johnny. It was a swell time while it lasted. If we're canned, we'll go to China. They'll make the three of us generals."

Suddenly, Johnny Kerrigan snapped his fingers. "*Generals!* That's it! I knew there was something I had to remember!"

He popped out of bed, and limped on his wounded leg to the closet. He fumbled in his coat pocket, came back with the small pin he had taken from one of the dead men in Kimber's Bar and Grill. He showed this to the other two.

Steve Klaw and Dan Murdoch were pretty well recovered from their burns, but they had asked the doctor to leave their bandages on in the hope that sympathy for their condition might restrain the Director from really going to town on them when he visited the hospital today.

They sat up without much difficulty, examining the pin.

Steve Klaw peered at it through his mummy bandages, whistled. "It's the badge of the Army of Death!"

Johnny Kerrigan nodded. "Kimber told me he was working for the General."

ALL THREE recalled whispers, which had been going the rounds for months, that a genius of criminal organization had arisen in the underworld, who called himself the 'General,' and who aspired to build an army of criminals which would be powerful enough to checkmate the F.B.I.

Rumors said that the gang leaders of a dozen large cities had been bludgeoned into joining the Army of Death. Here was proof that Kimber's murderous outfit were already enrolled. Several times recently, Kerrigan and Murdoch and Klaw had begged the Director to assign them the job of tracking down the Army of Death. But the Director had steadfastly refused—for the reason that he was extremely reluctant to assign them to *any* job unless absolutely compelled. Kerrigan had once punched a senator's son in the nose. Murdoch had shot a croupier to death in a gun duel in a crooked gambling house—where he shouldn't have been at all. And Steve Klaw had told a Senate investigating committee to go to hell because he didn't like the tone in which he was questioned as to why he had shot to kill in a gunfight with three bandits instead of trying to capture them. Any other agents who had committed such heinous offenses would have found themselves out of a job the next day. But Kerrigan and Murdoch and Klaw had records which few men could equal. The public would never have stood for their dismissal. So the Director, secretly glad of an excuse to the powers-that-be for not firing them, kept them on the payroll. But he used them only for those cases which he was reluctant to ask the other agents to undertake. And so Kerrigan, Murdoch and Klaw became the unofficial Suicide Squad of the F.B.I. Johnny Kerrigan took back the button of the Army of Death from Steve Klaw, and proudly pinned it on his pajamas.

"It looks," Steve said through his bandages, "like we were up against a pretty tough outfit that night. We had no right to come out alive."

"Never mind about coming out alive," said Dan Murdoch. "What'll we tell the boss when he comes? We're guilty of everything in the book—even to using department grenades without authorization. I would never have thrown the damn thing if they hadn't started to streak for the door. I let them go, figuring I'd be able to go up and give you two blokes a hand. But when they got out, they started to pepper me with slugs from the doorway. So I simply eased the grenade out among them."

Steve Klaw chuckled. "You looked awful funny, sitting under

the table, with a mug of beer perched on your dome, and the flames licking at you." He stopped as the door knob rattled.

Dan Murdoch hurriedly stuck his cigarette under the blanket, and Johnny Kerrigan leaped into his bed.

It was only the nurse, with an envelope. She smiled at them. "This is addressed to Messrs. Kerrigan, Murdoch and Klaw. Who wants it?"

Johnny Kerrigan put out his hand for it, and she gave it to him, left the room.

Klaw and Murdoch watched while he ripped open the envelope and extracted a large yellow sheet. He looked it over, whistled. Then he got out of bed and came over between Dan's and Steve's beds, and showed it to them.

At the top there was a printed emblem representing a man in shirt sleeves, with two swords crossed in front of him. Underneath was printed:

HEADQUARTERS ARMY OF DEATH

Beneath the heading was a typewritten message:

General Order to All Division Commanders:

WHEREAS: The three F.B.I. Agents, Kerrigan, Murdoch and Klaw have willfully killed a member of this Army, to wit, Russ Kimber, together with several of his men, and

WHEREAS: All members of the Army of Death are entitled to full protection and vengeance,

NOW THEREFORE: It is ordered that a reward of fifty thousand dollars be placed upon the body of each of the aforesaid men, and that they shall each and severally be marked for death. Any member of the Army of Death who delivers to his District or Division Commander the body of Kerrigan, Murdoch or Klaw—dead or alive—shall receive a cash reward of fifty thousand dollars, and shall also be promoted to Sub-Commander.   Signed,

THE GENERAL

Underneath this startling notice there was a further type-written postscript:

Kerrigan, Murdoch and Klaw:

Just as the F.B.I., posts "wanted" notices for so-called criminals, we are posting a reward for your bodies. Now you shall know what it means to be hunted men.

Your hours of life are numbered. You shall serve as examples to all others who may wish to molest the members of the Army of Death!

"Great stuff," said Dan Murdoch dreamily. "I hope it isn't a practical joke. I bet it would be real fun to have a reward on our heads!"

They heard voices in the corridor outside, and Johnny Kerrigan leaped back into bed.

THIS TIME it wasn't a false alarm. The Director had arrived. He stood for a minute just inside the door, and looked the three of them over.

Johnny Kerrigan groaned realistically, as if in great pain. Dan Murdoch squirmed in his bed. Steve Klaw croaked a husky "Good morning, sir," through his bandages.

The Director's face was inscrutable. "A fine bunch of sissies you turned out to be!" he growled. "Suicide Squad—bah! Letting yourselves get invalided by a bunch of hoodlums!"

His scowl became fiercer. "If you men weren't so sick, I'd have plenty to say to you. What right did you have to go into Kimber's place like that? What right did you have to use a Bureau grenade? Do you realize that I'm being subjected to pressure to fire you all?"

Johnny Kerrigan groaned again. "It was all my fault, sir. Frank Robbins is a friend of mine. He begged me to do what I could for him."

"So you staged a minor war!" the Director snorted. "I suppose you men are too sick to report for duty?"

"Duty?" There was a gleam in the two eyes of Steve Klaw, which were all that was visible of his face. "Have you an assignment for us, sir?"

The Director shrugged. "I was thinking of giving you a little job. Evidence has been piling up that this organization known as the Army of Death is more than a rumor. You've asked for permission to handle it. I assigned a detail of men last week, and all four of then have mysteriously disappeared. I thought maybe I'd let you three take it."

He sighed. "It's too bad you're all incapacitated. Well, I'll be down stairs in the superintendent's office for a few minutes. Take care of yourselves—so you'll be strong enough to take your medicine when you recover!"

He waved to them. There was a twinkle in his eyes as he turned and went out.

For a long minute after his departure utter silence filled the hospital room. Then anyone who looked in might have witnessed a strange sight—the spectacle of two wounded men and one mummy scrambling out of bed and throwing on their clothes with furious speed.

Within six minutes, a strange procession was running—not walking—down the hospital corridor. Dan Murdoch and Johnny Kerrigan looked like stuffed kewpie dolls, due to the fact that they had put their clothing on over their voluminous bandages. Steve Klaw resembled some weird apparition out of an Egyptian nightmare, for he had not removed the mummy-wrappings from his head and face. Only his eyes showed.

The three of them trooped into the superintendent's office, and came to attention facing the Director.

Steve Klaw was the spokesman.

"Kerrigan and Murdoch and Klaw reporting for duty, sir!" he said.

CHAPTER 4
SONS OF HELL

THE OFFICES of J. Augustus—Efficiency Expert, occupied the entire third and fourth floors of the old, out-moded Realty Building. The ground-floor store was tenanted by the Rialto Auctioneers, a flashy, blatant auction room where cheap jewelry and assorted job lots were sold to a credulous public at outrageously high prices. The second and fifth floors were vacant, and large "To Let" signs were plastered over the windows, preventing anyone from looking inside from the nearby buildings.

The windows of J. Augustus, on the third and fourth floors, were all equipped with Venetian blinds, rendering it likewise impossible to see what went on in those sumptuous offices. And strangely enough, whenever a prospective tenant inquired about renting the vacant second or fifth floors, he was quoted such a high rental that he didn't even bother to go up and look.

Thus, complete privacy was assured for the operations of J. Augustus.

Anyone with an inquiring mind, however, who took the pains to check up, would have noticed that many people who entered the building never seemed to come out again. Further investigation would have revealed a secret exit from one of the offices on the third floor. This exit led out on to the roof of a two-story taxicab garage in back of the Realty Building, with an entrance on the next street.

There was something worthy of note about this taxicab garage, too. The sign on the front of the building read:

GOLD STAR TAXICAB FLEET

And though there were at least two hundred of their black-and-gold taxicabs on the streets, it was never possible for an outside applicant to obtain a job—not even as a relief driver. In fact, no one was ever admitted into the building. Two men stood on guard day and night at the door, their sole purpose apparently to turn away applicants for jobs. And very often, when the black-and-gold cabs rolled out of the garage, it might have been noticed that their flags were already down, signifying that they were hired.

In fact, the Gold Star outfit was the envy of the other taxicab operators of the city, for they seemed to have a lot of private calls, and did not need to cruise the streets for patrons.

Whether by design or by accident, one of these black-and-gold taxicabs was waiting outside the Therapeutic Hospital on the very morning when Kerrigan and Murdoch and Klaw arose so precipitously from their beds to report for duty.

The flag was down, and the driver resolutely refused all passengers, declaring that he was waiting for a fare. This driver was a heavy-set, swarthy-faced individual, with a livid scar across his left cheek. Sitting at the wheel, he kept his gaze tensely fixed on the hospital entrance.

Suddenly he straightened in his seat, for he saw the lithe, boyish figure of Stephen Klaw emerge. Steve's face was still swathed in the mummy-bandages, so that only the eyes showed.

For a moment, the cab driver's eyes expressed doubt. He seemed to be expecting that Steve would not be alone. But when he saw that no one else came out, he shrugged, put up the flag. Then he tooled the cab forward abreast of the hospital entrance, reached back and opened the door.

"Cab, sir?" he asked.

Stephen Klaw's bandage-swathed head nodded. He got in and said, "Fifty-two East Ninetieth Street"—giving the address of Frank Robbins. Then he settled back in the cab, oblivious of the stares of several passers-by, who wondered what a mummy might be doing in a taxicab.

The cab started, and Steve leaned back in his seat, hands in his coat pockets. His eyes behind the bandages darted to right and left, watchful and keen. He turned and glanced behind, through the back window.

Kerrigan and Murdoch were supposed to be following him in a Bureau car. But they were not there.

In the hospital, they had decided on a course of action typical of their bold and reckless natures. Since the General had marked them for death, they would give him a chance to try. One of them would stick his chin out for it. The other two would be in the background, ready to step in.

As always when there was a choice of dangers, they had tossed. And once again little Stephen Klaw had won. He was to be the spearhead....

KERRIGAN AND Murdoch watched him go down the hospital steps and get into the black-and-gold taxi. "The little shrimp always gets the breaks!" Dan Murdoch said sourly. "Come on, Johnny. Let's get on his tail, quick. We don't want anything to happen to that mummy!"

They hurried out to the side entrance, where the F.B.I. car was waiting for them, with a Bureau chauffeur. It would only be a matter of seconds to swing around the corner, and take up the trail of the black-and-gold cab.

They came running out of the building, and Johnny Kerrigan waved to the chauffeur. The chauffeur saw them coming and climbed quickly into the car, stepping on the starter.

Kerrigan and Murdoch were still twenty feet away.

A closed truck, which had been parked down the street,

suddenly accelerated into motion. It roared past them. And as it passed, two peepholes in the side came open. A machine-gun barrel was thrust out of each. At once the whole street was filled with the deadly din and clatter of those two rapid-firers. Hot lead swept along the side of the Bureau car, and smashed into the walls and windows of the hospital.

Kerrigan and Murdoch acted with the instantaneous reactions of trained fighting men. Even before the machine-guns began to chatter, they threw themselves prone on the sidewalk, under the shelter of the armored F.B.I. car.

The truck raced past with its vicious hail of death, and pulled up fifty feet away, with screaming brakes. The guns stopped hammering. Its driver maneuvered it around. It was clear that he intended to make a complete turn and come back for another broadside.

Kerrigan and Murdoch were already on their feet, firing steadily and methodically at the truck. But their bullets glanced harmlessly off the sides. It was armored.

The truck was halfway around.

"We can't stop him with bullets, Johnny!" Murdoch shouted.

Kerrigan nodded.

Their driver was slumped at the wheel, blood spurting from his neck and head. His window had been open, and he had taken the fusillade full in the head.

Kerrigan's lips were tight, thin. He climbed in and pulled the driver over, got behind the wheel. Dan Murdoch stood on the running-board, swiftly reloading his gun.

In spite of his wounded leg, Johnny Kerrigan got the big

F.B.I. car in motion before the truck was turned all the way around. He slipped it in first, and stepped all the way down on the gas.

The big car shot like an arrow, straight for the front part of the slowly turning truck.

The driver of the truck saw that catapult coming, and his mouth dropped open. Frantically he twisted at the wheel to avoid the collision. The truck shot forward at an angle across the street, climbed the curb, and crashed head-on into the building opposite.

Johnny Kerrigan, laughing deeply and bitterly, stepped hard on the brake as the F.B.I. car slipped past the tail of the truck, barely missing it.

The driver of the truck had been thrown forward, and his head had split against the windshield. But the two machine-gunners inside the truck were evidently more frightened than hurt.

The rear door came open precipitately, and they leaped out, still carrying their tommy-guns. They started to run, then saw that Murdoch and Kerrigan were already out of the Bureau car and racing toward them.

Snarling like cornered beasts, they turned now and raised their lethal 'typewriters.'

Johnny Kerrigan, whose gun was empty, kept on running toward them, his face hot with fury.

But Dan Murdoch stopped. Coolly, deliberately, he swung up his revolver. He fired once, twice. The two gunmen dropped. Murdoch's shooting was deadly accurate. They were dead before they hit the ground.

Kerrigan and Murdoch did not spare a glance at the two. They looked at each other.

"The rats killed our driver," said Johnny.

Dan nodded. "And they made us lose Steve. God knows now what the shrimp is up against!"

STEPHEN KLAW was already a block away in the black-and-gold taxicab. He distinctly heard the *rat-tat-tat* of the machine-guns, and the deeper thunder of Kerrigan's and Murdoch's thirty-eights.

He tapped on the partition glass.

"Turn back!" he ordered the driver.

The driver gave no acknowledgment of his order. Instead, he swung west at the next corner. Even if he had not heard he should be going east instead of west.

Stephen Klaw grew taut. He said nothing to the driver, but reached out, tried the door. It would not open. He moved over, grasped the left-hand door handle. It, too, was locked from the outside.

Klaw's eyes were two sparkling points in the recesses of the bandage. He bent forward and brought out one of his automatics from his coat pocket. He reversed it, struck a resounding blow with the butt against the partition glass in front. The glass did not break.

The driver slowed down to a crawl. He turned and looked over his shoulder. He was grinning as if over a huge joke.

Stephen Klaw raised his automatic and fired into the glass, straight at the driver's face. The glass splintered, but did not break. The lead slug glanced off it and ricocheted into the uphol-stery.

The driver laughed, and put a thumb to his nose. He brought the cab to a stop, and bent down and adjusted something along-side his seat, which Steve could not see. Then he climbed out.

He made a mocking salute, and calmly crossed the street. Then he turned around to watch.

Steve looked at him puzzled. They were parked a block from the river, alongside vacant lots. The driver across the street lit a cigarette and waved sardonically.

Steve Klaw got up and peered through the partition glass. He saw that there was a small phonograph on the floor alongside of the seat, and there was a record on the turntable.

It was that phonograph which the driver had adjusted before getting out. Steve also noticed, with dispassionate interest, that the driver had left the motor running.

Almost at once, a voice began speak. It was emanating from the radio in the cab, and he realized that the phonograph was connected with it.

"Attention, Mr. G-man—or men; I don't know how many of you my driver has trapped in the cab. But whether there are one, or two, or three of you—you have exactly sixty seconds to live. There is a time-bomb attached underneath the chassis of this car, hooked up to the battery, which you cannot reach. When my voice ceases speaking on this record, the timing apparatus of the bomb, which is connected to the fan of the motor, will be set in motion. Thirty seconds after I sign off the bomb will explode. It contains one pound of tri-nitro-toluene. Do you understand? *One pound.* I am giving you the extra thirty seconds to reflect upon your rashness in opposing the Army of Death. This, gentlemen, is the General—*signing off!*"

The voice ceased speaking.

Steve Klaw looked at his wrist watch, started watching the second-hand.

"Chalk up one for the General!" he said.

He raised his automatic and emptied it into the glass window. The gun thundered in the close confines of the cab, almost deafening him. The smell of burnt powder became thick and choking. But the laminated glass resisted the bullets. It cracked, and the cracks spread in a spider-web. But it did not break.

Steve shrugged, threw the gun away. Then he waved airily to the driver, who was watching him from the opposite side.

The driver grinned, and gave him an ironic bow. He was waiting there to watch the end of Stephen Klaw.

Steve looked at his wrist watch. Eight seconds to go.

"This is a hell of a way to die!" he muttered, and started to strip the bandages from his face.

CHAPTER 5
DEATH TO THE F.B.I.

O N T H E third door of the old Realty Building, twelve men were gathered in a large office. They were seated around a directors' table, with cigars and cocktails at their disposal.

The heart of any law-enforcement officer in the land might

have stirred with foreboding at sight of those twelve. For they were the kingpins of crime in widely separated parts of the country.

From Chicago, Big Mike Pellucci had come in a chartered private car. Jake Cadman, thin and vinegary, and vicious as a cobra, had driven to this meeting from Milwaukee in an armored sedan. Lou Sorgum, bald-headed and calculating, had flown from Frisco in his own plane. From Miami and Pittsburgh and Duluth and Baltimore, the others had come to gather here at this hour.

They had all come in through the Gold Star Garage in the back street, and had been conducted to this room. And in spite of the fact that each was armed; that each had bodyguards waiting near by; in spite of the liquor and cigars provided them, all felt ill at ease.

When the door at the far end of the room opened without warning, they jerked nervously. Then a sigh escaped from them, as if in chorus.

A tall man stood in the doorway. He was powerfully built. His bearing bespoke self-assurance.

It was his face, however, that attracted all their eyes, like a magnet. That face was lined and creased. The lips were thin, hard, cruel. And in the depths of his eyes those twelve men read a capacity for evil to which even they had never dared.

All recognized him.

"Gus Jarger!" gasped Lou Sorgum.

The man by the doorway inclined his head. A faint smile of

contempt flicked at his lips. "Augustus Jarger—in person, gentle-men. Now doing business as J. Augustus!"

Who in that room did not know Augustus Jarger! Ten years ago he had ruled a stupendous empire of crime, with ramifications in dozens of cities. At his word, men had died under machine-gun bullets, or encased in concrete at the river bottom. But, where local law had failed, the F.B.I. had caught up with him. He had gone to Alcatraz for ten years. He was eligible for parole in seven, but had viciously refused such clemency.

"I'll owe nothing to anybody!" he had snarled to his lawyer, and would not sign the parole application. "I've learned my lesson. When I come out, they'll hear from me. I'll laugh in their faces. I'll make the F.B.I. pay for these ten years—in blood. And no living man will be able to lay a finger on me!"

So they said that Gus Jarger was going crazy in stir. They said that he had softening of the brain. When Jarger's time was up, he walked out of jail and disappeared. They thought that was the end of him.

It was not....

Now his faintly contemptuous glance rested, in turn, on each of those twelve nervous men.

"You are here today because you have no choice," he said. "You found your rackets going to hell in each city that you control. Your gorillas were killed in mysterious fashion, your hideouts bombed."

He stopped talking, came slowly up to the table. Then he leaned slightly forward.

"Gentlemen, *I* did all that to you. From now on, not one

of you will operate independently. I am the General. You are subordinates in the Army of Death. I already have fifty cities in line. Your twelve cities are the last of the larger ones. With you twelve as part of the Army of Death, we will have an organization greater than anything in the world. We will have a gross annual income of four billion dollars. We will be able to smash everything in our path—including the Federal Bureau of Investigation. We will be able to elect mayors and governors and congressmen. Who knows—maybe even the President!"

When he paused, a ripple of gasps went round the table.

"W-what do we get for joining up?" Jake Cadman asked.

J. Augustus fixed his eyes on Cadman. "What do you get? Ask rather what I will give you. I will dispense all the rewards. I will divide the income. In return, you will be assured that no one can molest you. You will carry out my orders in each of your cities, without opposition. Anyone who stands in your way will be removed at once. You heard how Kerrigan, Murdoch and Klaw shot up Russ Kimber's outfit. Well, those three G-men are living on borrowed time from this moment on. There's a price on their heads. I aim to make the Army of Death as feared by law officers as the F.B.I. has been feared by criminals. And all of you will enjoy the protection of the Army of Death!"

They stirred uneasily. In their vicious and venomous hearts they were enthralled by the picture of power which J. Augustus had painted. They would have been willing to acknowledge him as their overlord—provided they were certain he could deliver. But they still remembered those rumors that Gus Jarger had gone nuts in stir.

Mike Pellucci voiced the secret sentiment. "You're loco, Jarger. Nobody can do what you claim. You can't buck the whole United States government—"

"You are mistaken, Pellucci. It can be done," was the answer. "Up to the present, the F.B.I. has had little opposition worthy of its mettle. Hoodlums, illiterates like most of you—who work without real plan or organization—are easily licked. We will see what the much vaunted F.B.I. can do when it is opposed by a real efficiency expert of crime—plus an ability to organize along military lines. We can't fail, Pellucci."

"I still think you're nuts!" Mike Pellucci said stubbornly.

"It doesn't matter what you think. You must join the Army of Death. You have no choice."

"And what if I refuse?"

"I advise you not to refuse."

"To hell with you!" said Big Mike. "I'll run my own town in my own way. Now I know who's been throwing the monkey wrench in the works, I'll put a quick stop to it—"

J. Augustus raised a hand.

"I'm sorry, Pellucci. There's no room for you any more. You must be liquidated."

He nodded once, as if in signal. There was a *popping* sound from one side of the room, and a puff of smoke.

Big Mike threw his arms out in a dreadful, frantic gesture. His mouth dropped open in frightful ludicrous fashion. Blood spurted from a wound in his heart. Slowly he crumpled and fell across the table.

From an opening in the paneled wall, a rifle barrel protruded, with a silencer screwed on the end. Little wisps of smoke spiraled up from the muzzle.

The eleven men at the table stared at that rifle in stunned silence.

J. Augustus smiled thinly. "Is there any one else," he asked silkily, "who wishes to raise objections?"

Each one shook his head violently in the negative.

"Excellent," said J. Augustus. "If some one will please push Pellucci's body off the table, we can make our final arrangements. You must all return to your home cities at once. Tomorrow at noontime is the zero hour. At zero hour we shall launch our campaign throughout the country. You will all have instructions. The first blow will be to smash the F.B.I. Then we take over the country!"

CHAPTER 6
SPECIAL AGENTS
FOR MURDER

EIGHT SECONDS are not much in the lifetime of a man. Yet many things can happen in that short span. In the Argentine, a baby is born; in Shantung a sentry is shot by a sniper; in Kwangsi a warplane is shattered by shrapnel high in the air; in Madrid a man standing blindfolded before a wall is riddled by the bullets of an execution squad. In the same eight seconds of time, men are born and die in all parts of the earth.

Yet it is too short a time for one man to make his peace with God.

But a man can have a thought in a fraction of a second. For a thought is not a thing, or even a word; but a flash—a God-given spark which can course through the convolutions of the mind with the speed of light. It is execution of the thought which takes the time. Eight seconds are hardly enough to convert thought into action.

Stephen Klaw understood this.

So when the thought came to him—how he could save himself from the tri-nitro bomb under the taxicab, he did nothing for a precious fraction of a second.

But because he was one of those who by nature must keep on fighting while there remained any chance at all, he swung swiftly into action. The bomb might go off while he was trying. But he couldn't ignore the chance.

He stopped stripping the bandages from his face.

And then, with hands which did not hurry too much, but which wasted no single motion, he raised his automatic and smashed out the glass covering the dome light in the roof of the cab. Then with swift fingers he unscrewed the small bulb and let it drop to the floor.

At the same time, his other hand was fishing a penny out of his pocket—a precious copper penny which was going to stand between himself and extermination… if there was time.

He thrust the penny up into the empty bulb socket, pressing it against the two terminals.

His wrist watch showed the eighth second.

There was a flash.

But it was not the explosion. It was the flash caused by the short-circuiting of the current through the penny. The ignition died. The motor jerked, and ceased to throb.

Stephen Klaw stood there with the penny in the socket, and waited. If the fan-belt continued a full revolution after the motor stopped, it would still acuate the timing-mechanism, and cause the bomb to explode. A half-second, a quarter-second, would tell the story.

Nothing happened.

Stephen Klaw let the penny drop out of the socket. He sighed through his bandages.

"Boy!" he whispered. "This is the second birth of Stephen Klaw!"

He turned around and looked across the street, where the driver with the scar on his face was beginning to look worried. Steve put a thumb to his nose in an expressive gesture. The man realized that the motor had stopped running. He knew now, that the bomb would not explode. His mouth twisted into a vicious line. A gun came out of his pocket. He dropped to one knee, and fired.

The shot clanged against metal somewhere under the car.

Steve Klaw understood. The man was aiming at the bomb. He was going to explode it with a shot. His eyes, through the bandage slit, showed nothing of what he felt. He merely rested his elbow on the window ledge, and his chin on his palm. He watched the driver's marksmanship with calm detachment.

The man aimed more carefully for the second shot. He was grinning as he aimed.

It was apparent from his look of confidence that he couldn't miss this time….

But he didn't fire the second shot, because a siren started to scream down at the corner. The driver turned to look.

Steve Klaw followed his glance. Steve's eyes sparkled. It was the F.B.I. car. He couldn't see who was driving it, but he saw Dan Murdoch on the running-board. He needed only one guess as to who was behind the wheel.

The car came careening down the street, and Dan Murdoch opened up with his revolver. The scar-faced driver yelled in panic and turned to run. The F.B.I. car raced past Steve's taxi, and caught the running driver, easily.

Johnny Kerrigan, at the wheel, slowed down, kept abreast of him, and honked.

The driver turned around, snarling, and began to shoot. Dan Murdoch, with no trace of expression on his face, shot him in the head.

Then Johnny Kerrigan brought the car to a stop, and they ran back to the taxicab. They stopped alongside it, and Johnny tried the door handle. It opened. The lock had been reversed, so that it locked from the outside instead of the inside.

Steve Klaw came out, still swathed in his mummy-bandages.

"Hiyah, Shrimp?" said Dan Murdoch.

"Hiyah, Shrimp?" echoed Johnny Kerrigan.

"Okay, mopes," said Stephen Klaw.

STEVE KLAW didn't give Kerrigan and Murdoch a chance to ask any questions. He ran around to the front of the cab and lifted off the record from the phonograph.

Kerrigan grinned. "What's that, Shrimp—a souvenir?"

"It's only made of wax," Steve told him. "But it'll hang somebody pretty soon!"

He looked swiftly up and down the street. Nobody was in sight yet.

"Come on, guys!" he ordered, and raced to the Bureau car. "Pile in," he said. "And take the wheel, Johnny!"

So accustomed were these three to working together, that no one asked questions. Kerrigan got behind the wheel, and Murdoch took the record from Steve, climbed in the back

Steve dropped to one knee, and took the automatic from his pocket. He squinted at the taxicab, saw the dark bulk of the tri-nitro bomb that was slung underneath.

"Hold your hats, boys!" he yelled, and fired once.

The bark of his shot was drowned by the thunderous detonation which blew up the taxicab. The street literally rocked under them, and they were deafened by the blast. The cab was dissolved into a million pieces of hurtling steel, upholstery and motor parts.

Shredded metal shot up into the air as if from a geyser, and then began to rain down upon them! Echoes of the terrific explosion rolled back from the river like the thunder of distant artillery.

Stephen Klaw hopped into the Bureau car. "Let's go, Johnny!"

Johnny Kerrigan sent the sedan flashing down the street, turned the corner and drove south along the river front for a half-dozen blocks. Then he pulled up. He glared at Steve Klaw, who was sitting innocently beside him.

"What's the gag, Shrimp? Why'd you blow that thing up? It was evidence."

Steve grinned. "I'm officially dead now. Your story will be that you got on the scene just one minute too late. You shot that driver, and then the cab exploded—with me in it."

Johnny Kerrigan nodded with dawning understanding. "So the General will think he's one up on us!"

"Right—and two to go. He'll concentrate on you two mopes. He won't be looking for me in the background."

"Not bad," said Murdoch. "Where do we go from here?"

"To the garage where that hack came from," Steve told him. "We'll see what makes the black-and-gold cabs go round!"

Johnny Kerrigan's eyes glittered. "Let's go!"

CHAPTER 7
FIGHTING IS MADE FOR FEDS

AN HOUR later, when the big Bureau car pulled up in front of the Gold Star Garage, only two men were to be seen in it. Johnny Kerrigan was at the wheel, and Dan Murdoch sat beside him. However, if the guard at the garage door had taken the trouble to look in the rear, he would have seen a suspiciously bulky object on the floor, covered by an auto robe.

Kerrigan swung the car right up on the ramp, and stopped with its nose touching the heavy chain slung across the entrance. Two guards who stood at the doorway, came around to the car, hands hovering close to their shoulders.

One was hard-faced, with a low forehead and bushy eyebrows. The other had thin, pinched features, a pointed chin.

"What do you want here?" Bushy-eyebrows demanded.

Johnny Kerrigan did not move from behind the wheel, but his hand dropped to the service revolver in his lap. "You take it from here, Dan," he said.

Dan Murdoch opened the door on his side, and got out. "We want in," he said.

Bushy-eyebrows scowled. "No strangers allowed, mister. Scram."

"Did you ever see one of these?" Murdoch asked mildly. He slowed his F.B.I. badge.

Bushy-eyebrows grew taut. He threw a quick glance at Pointy-chin, then turned back to Dan. "So what, mister? You still can't come in—without a search warrant."

"My friend in the car has the search warrant," Murdoch said. "Show them the search warrant, Johnny."

Johnny Kerrigan smiled broadly. He lifted up his service revolver, held it carelessly pointing at the two guards. "How do you like this for a search warrant, lugs? Want to put up an argument?"

In the moment that the two men turned to stare at the big muzzle of Johnny's gun, Dan Murdoch drew his own. He stepped behind the two men.

"An hour ago," he said, an odd, frosty deadliness in his voice, "one of your cabs picked up a friend of ours by the name of Stephen Klaw. It was blown to bits. It had a bomb planted in it. If you think I wouldn't shoot you down like a couple of rats, you're crazy."

Bushy-eyebrows began to shake. "Y-youse guys must be Kerrigan and Murdoch."

"That's right, friend. Steve Klaw was our partner."

"W-what do you want?"

"We're going in and ask a few questions of the manager. You can try to stop us—or not. It's all the same to us."

"We ain't stopping you, mister."

Dan Murdoch sighed almost regretfully. He stepped back, unhooked the chain, and nodded to Johnny Kerrigan, who drove the Bureau car into the garage. Then Dan motioned to the two guards. They marched inside under the muzzle of his gun.

Johnny tooled the car over into a dark corner at the rear of the garage, and climbed out. He left it facing out, with the motor running. Then he walked over to where Dan stood with Bushy-eyebrows and Pointy-chin. "Take us to the manager's office!"

The two gunmen were licked, scared stiff. Meekly they led the way to a staircase. "It's up at the head of the stairs," said Pointy-chin.

"What's the manager's name?" Murdoch asked.

"Lemson—Tony Lemson."

Dan Murdoch raised his eyebrows.

"I've heard of the guy. He used to be the boss of the taxi-cab rackets in Chicago. Then he was indicted, and got the case quashed—but he had to leave Chicago. I heard he was dead broke. Where'd he get the dough to go in this business?"

Bushy-eyebrows shrugged. "I wouldn't know."

Dan grinned. "Lemson wouldn't be financed by—say, the General, would he?"

He watched the two men carefully as he said it, and caught a tremor in the face of Pointy-chin.

"We wouldn't know," said Pointy-chin.

Johnny Kerrigan sighed. "I think we should work these two guys over a little, Dan, before we go up. Kind of shake up their memory."

Half a dozen cab drivers had moved over near them, watching with ill-concealed animosity. Dan Murdoch had pinned his F.B.I. badge on his coat lapel, so they all knew that these men were law officers. Besides, the efficient manner in which Johnny and Dan handled their artillery would have been enough to discourage them anyway. It was easy to see, though, that these drivers were more than mere hackmen. Their faces were hard-bitten, vicious.

But as vicious and dangerous as they were, they had no urge to face the two cold-eyed men who covered them. For word had somehow spread around the garage that Kerrigan and Murdoch were here—on the kill, to avenge their partner, Stephen Klaw. **JUST THEN** a hard, uncompromising voice spoke harshly from the head of the stairs. "What's going on here?" Tony Lemson, the manager, had come out of the office, and was standing at the top, close to the banister, gun in hand.

Johnny Kerrigan had seen him walk out of the office up there, but said nothing. He had merely moved over a bit, so that he had a clear shot up the stairs in case of trouble.

"Here's the guy we want, Dan!" he said, and started up the stairs.

Dan Murdoch nodded. He leaned back negligently against the wall, eyeing the ugly-faced drivers. "Make it short and snappy, Johnny," he called up to his partner.

Tony Lemson scowled down at the ascending Kerrigan. He raised his gun a little. "Stop where you are!" he ordered. "You got no right in here. Take another step up, and I'll shoot you. I'm within my rights!"

Johnny Kerrigan grinned happily, and kept advancing. "Looks like some real opposition, for a change. You think you can shoot to kill, Lemson? It'll be too bad, if you miss."

He said it genially, like some one giving brotherly advice. But Tony Lemson, looking down at him, met his cold eyes, and gulped. He licked his lips.

"I don't want no trouble with you guys. You got no right coming in here without a warrant. I'll call the cops."

That was as far as he got, because Johnny Kerrigan was already at the top step. The big G-man just reached out with the flat of his hand and pushed Lemson in the face. The manager staggered backward, through the open door of his office. Johnny came after him, and caught a bunch of his coat in one huge paw. He shook the man like a rat.

"Use that gun," he said coolly, "or drop it!"

Lemson let the gun fall.

"That's better," said Johnny, and released his grip on the manager's coat.

Lemson was gasping for breath. "You damn gorilla! You can't come in here and use strong-arm stuff. I'll have you fired."

Johnny holstered his service revolver, and hit Lemson with his fist. He hit him in the mouth, sending him smashing into the desk.

Lemson's lip started to bleed. He put up a hand to ward off another blow. His voice lost all its bluster. "Lay off me!" he whined. "I'm clean, so help me!"

Johnny Kerrigan laughed harshly. "Clean? It was one of your cabs that exploded an hour ago. Stephen Klaw was in that cab. A bomb was rigged in it. It wasn't your fault that you didn't get all three of us."

"I swear I don't know what you're talking about!" Lemson gasped. "I—I heard about the cab being blown up. But I don't know about no bomb. Somebody musta thrown it."

"Nobody threw it. It was planted in the cab. It was your cab. You know who planted that bomb. You're going to tell me— now."

Lemson licked his lips. He looked at Johnny Kerrigan's solid bulk, shivered. He was as big as Johnny—but he wasn't thinking of putting up a fight.

"I swear I had nothing to do with it. Maybe the driver did it on his own."

"Come on," said Johnny. "I'm taking you in—as a material witness. You'll talk before tonight!" He took Lemson by the arm, dragged him roughly out to the stairhead.

Down below, Bushy-eyebrows and Pointy-chin were standing in a huddle with the rest of the tough drivers, watching Dan Murdoch sharply.

Johnny grinned down at Dan. "What—no action yet?"

Murdoch shrugged. "The rats won't start anything."

Kerrigan nudged Tony Lemson down the stairs to the garage floor. "We're taking Lemson in as a material witness," he announced. "Anybody want to stop us?"

"What the hell!" exclaimed Bushy-eyebrows. "We can take these two guys."

"Shut up, Marko!" Tony Lemson spat through his bleeding lips. "Don't you see these guys are on the kill? They're just looking for an excuse!"

Dan Murdoch laughed. "That's right, Marko," he said softly. "Just an excuse. Any *little* excuse will do!"

The bushy-browed Marko shrank within himself as he saw the look on Dan Murdoch's face.

Kerrigan snapped handcuffs on Lemson, pushed him out to the street. Dan Murdoch backed out after him. Marko and the others followed slowly, watching for a possible opening. Murdoch gave them none. He kept facing them while Kerrigan cuffed Tony Lemson to the coat rack behind the front seat, got behind the wheel.

"Okay, Dan," he said calmly.

Murdoch backed into the sedan, constantly facing the crew of drivers in the doorway.

SO ABSORBED were Marko and the cab drivers, that they did not notice what was going on inside the garage, behind their backs.

The suspicious-looking bundle in the rear of the Bureau car had suddenly come to life. The rug which covered it was shucked off, and a man climbed out of the car. This man's face had four long scars on it, apparently caused by severe burns which had not completely healed as yet. One was across the forehead, two on the right cheek, and one along the right side of the jaw. They did not look very pretty, but they served a very useful purpose, for they made the face of Stephen Klaw unrecognizable to anybody not expecting to see him—for instance, anybody who might have thought him dead.

Taking advantage of the fact that all the men in the garage were at the door watching Kerrigan and Murdoch, Steve Klaw slipped along the wall, then upstairs. He grinned as he noted that Johnny and Dan were taking their time about pulling away with their prisoner. They were giving him as much opportunity as possible to get up the stairs without being observed.

The whole idea of invading the garage had been solely to get Steve Klaw planted in there. They had known in advance that, if the garage was really headquarters for a gang working under the directions of the General, it would be impossible to make any of the men talk. Much more could be accomplished, they hoped, by getting inside, unobserved.

Steve Klaw saw the open door of Lemson's office, but did not go in. He moved down the hall, with his hands in his coat pockets, wary lest there be any more gunmen up here. He heard the Bureau car accelerating as it drove away. Then came the voices of Marko and the others, returning inside. There was a grinding, rasping noise…. The rolling doors of the garage were being shut, to keep out any other possible intruders. These men did not intend to be caught napping a second time.

Stephen Klaw stopped in the hall and listened, to see if any of the men might be coming up. But at the moment they were apparently too busy conversing in excited voices.

Steve smiled. Kerrigan and Murdoch had put the fear of God in them. He'd have a few minutes to investigate.

There were four more doors along this hall, after the open door of Lemson's office. Then there was an iron ladder leading up to a skylight in the roof. Past the ladder was a big iron fire-door. Steve inched this open, saw that it led to the second-floor storage space of the garage. There were thirty or forty black-and-gold taxicabs up here, and in the front of the building was a repair shop where several mechanics worked on cars.

Steve closed the fire-door carefully, making no noise. Then he turned his attention to the other doors along the hall.

The first door was locked, with the key on the *outside*. Steve's eyes glittered. He turned the key carefully, pushed the door open. Then he stopped stock-still on the threshold, his eyes narrowed to mere slits.

CHAPTER 8
DIE—AND BE DAMNED!

THERE WAS an army cot in the room, up against one wall. A man lay on the cot. He wore only an undershirt and trousers. There was a crude bandage around his head, another across his stomach. The undershirt had been pulled up on his

105

chest to make room for the bandage, and had not been pulled down again. Blood was on both bandages.

It was not that which held Stephen Klaw's attention, however. It was the face of the semiconscious man. His features had been battered almost to a pulp. Both eyes were closed and swollen, the nose broken. His lips were split, and there were long gashes down both of his checks, from which blood was now seeping.

As the man heard Steve step into the room, he groaned. Then feeble words came from his bleeding mouth.

"To hell with you all. You can beat me to death. I won't make the phone call…."

Stephen Klaw closed the door softly behind him, and came up to the cot. There was a terrible look of cold fury in his slate-gray eyes. He knew this man. "What have they been doing to you, Daly?" he asked.

The man tried to raise himself on his elbow. "Damn you," he croaked. "I tell you I won't make the call, I won't trap my brother officers. You can kill me by inches…."

"Take it easy, Daly," said Steve Klaw. "Nobody's going to kill you. Nobody's going to hurt you—not any more!"

Daly was one of the four Special Agents of the Federal Bureau of Investigation who had first been assigned to investigate the Army of Death—then, like the other three, had disappeared without leaving a clue. Where the other three were, it was easy to guess. And the fiends had been working on Daly, trying to force him to make a phone call. Steve could also guess what kind of phone call they had wanted him to make.

He dropped to his knees beside the cot. "This is Steve Klaw. Take it easy, and you'll be all right. I'll get you out of here."

Daly's blackened eyes and bleeding face were expressive of the tortures he had undergone. He was done for. Steve knew, looking at him, that he would never live. But he tried to make himself sound cheerful.

"I'll get you to a hospital."

Daly's voice, strangled and gasping, interrupted him. "No use, Klaw. I'm… through. That General… look out for him. A devil. His name is Gus… Augustus…."

Special Agent Daly's voice trailed off into a hacking rattle. Blood gushed from his mouth. He grew limp, and his mouth fell open. He was not dead yet, but death was probably only a short distance away.

"I promise you I'll get the General!" Steve said grimly.

He held on to Daly's hand for almost five minutes. He was aware of motion outside in the hall, of voices and footsteps. There was always danger now of some one noticing that the key had disappeared from outside the door. Men might come.

But Stephen Klaw was oblivious of everything. He knelt beside Gregg Daly, held his hand until the final spasm of death contracted the unfortunate man's body. Then he slowly and reverently crossed his hands on his chest, pulled a sheet over him.

He stood up, came to attention before the body. His eyes were hard, lips grim.

"Gregg Daly," he said, "I'll square accounts for you. I'll get the General!"

HE TURNED and made for the door. He was about to open it, when he heard voices on the other side. Marko and Pointy-chin were talking. "I've got to go over and ask the Boss what to do," Marko was saying.

"The Boss is in conference," Pointy-chin replied. "Those twelve guys ain't gone yet. He won't like to be disturbed."

"For *this* he won't mind being disturbed," Marko said. "We can't stay closed up forever. There'll be cabs coming back. We got to let them in. And we got to get Lemson sprung before Kerrigan and Murdoch tear him to pieces."

Steve Klaw's eyes were glittering, as he listened.

"Okay," Pointy-chin agreed. "Go ahead. I'll go in and see if that G-man is dead yet. If he ain't, maybe I can work him over a little. He can't stand a whole lot more. Maybe he'll weaken and make that phone call."

Stephen Klaw heard Marko's heavy footsteps receding. He listened carefully, but did not hear the opening of the fire door at the end of the hall. Instead, he thought he detected the scraping of shoes against iron—*moving upward.*

Then he heard Marko's voice from somewhere above in the hall, speaking to Pointy-chin, "Don't use the sap on him no more, Smiley. You'll kill him for sure. Try burning his toes."

"Okay," chuckled the pointy-chinned Smiley.

Stephen Klaw stood tautly behind the door. He heard Marko's heavy feet scraping on iron. He knew now where Marko was going—*up that ladder.* That was the way to the Boss. What was it Daly had said with his dying breath—*Gus… Augustus?* Had he given the General's full name, or had he been trying to utter a last name when he died?

Steve had no more time for speculation, because he saw the knob turn, as Smiley started to come in. Then he saw the knob stop turning, heard a muttered ejaculation on the other side of the door. Smiley must have discovered that the key was missing.

Stephen Klaw yanked the door open. He grinned into Smiley's startled face, took one of the automatics out of a pocket. "Come in, Smiley," he said softly. "Come right in!"

Smiley's pointed chin dropped as his mouth fell open. His face turned a ghastly green. Klaw reached out and caught him by the coat, pulled hard. Smiley came tumbling into the room and Steve let go of him and sent him sprawling on the floor. Then he closed the door, locked it. When he turned around, Smiley was on his knees, dragging a gun out of a shoulder holster.

Green fire flashed in Steve Klaw's eyes. He took a quick step forward, and kicked hard at Smiley's hand. There was a sharp snap as the wrist-bone broke.

Smiley yelled with pain, and fell on his face, hugging his shattered wrist. The gun fell to the floor.

Steve kicked the gun out of the way. "Get up!" he said tonelessly.

Smiley yelled again, raising his voice so that the men downstairs could hear him. "Hey, guys—"

It was all he was able to get out, because Steve Klaw bent down, wrapped fingers around his throat and squeezed the wind out of him. Steve held the throat until Smiley's face began to grow purple. Then he let go.

"Get up!" he said.

Smiley whimpered with pain, but got to his feet. "Gawd! My hand—"

STEVE GRINNED evilly, thrust him forward until he was standing close to the cot upon which lay the dead body of Gregg Daly. "So you were going to work him over some more, eh? You used a sap on his face, didn't you? You beat his face to a pulp, trying to force him to make a phone call. And now you were going to burn his toes, weren't you?"

He smashed a fist to Smiley's face, sending him to the floor.

"Take off your shoes and socks!" he ordered.

"W-what you gonna do?"

"Give you the same treatment you were going to give poor Daly. Burn your toes off. Like the idea?"

"Gawd, no! Give us a break—"

"Sure. Sure," Klaw said. "I'll give you the same kind of break you gave Daly. I'll leave you here to die—after I finish with you!"

"Gawd, mister, I'll do anything. *Anything*. Only give me a break. I got a weak heart. I'll die!"

"Not too soon, I hope," Klaw said. "Take off your shoes and socks—or I'll tie you up and take them off myself."

Smiley's trembling hands began to fumble with his shoe laces.

"Maybe," Steve said thoughtfully, "I'll lay off you—if you sing a nice song."

The thug's pointed chin actually wiggled in excitement. "Yes, mister. I'll sing. I'll talk. Anything. Anything you wanta know!"

"All right. Start talking. Who's the General?"

"Gawd, mister, I don't know. Only the big shots in the outfit know. Marko knows—and the guys who run the other cities."

"How do you get to the General?" Klaw demanded.

"Over the roof."

There was a queer, cunning look in Smiley's eyes. "You cross over to the old building in back. It's the old Realty Building. You press a button, and a door opens in the wall. After that I don't know what you do. I never went through that door."

Steve didn't seem to notice Smiley's look of cunning. He pressed on with his questions. "What kind of a phone call were you trying to force Daly to make?"

"We were gonna have him call the F.B.I. office and ask for Kerrigan or Murdoch," was the answer. "He was to say that he was a prisoner in a cellar down the street, under the Greek restaurant near the corner. The cellar is wired with a couple of bombs. When Kerrigan and Murdoch open a door or window, they get blown to pieces."

"I see," said Stephen Klaw. He motioned to Smiley. "Take off your belt."

He used Smiley's belt to strap his arms to his sides. Then he took the sheet off Daly's body, and tore it in half. He put half back on the dead man. The other half he tore into strips. He used these to tie Smiley's wrists and ankles and gag him cruelly.

Smiley fainted with the pain when he tied strips on his wrists, but Klaw went right ahead. When he had him well trussed up, he left him on the floor and went out, taking the key. He locked the door on the outside, but put the key in his pocket instead of leaving it in the door.

There was nobody in the hall. He looked up, and saw that Marko had left a trapdoor open in the roof. It was through that trapdoor that he had climbed out, and the fact that he left it open indicated that he intended to return soon.

STEPHEN KLAW went back to the open door of Lemson's office. Standing in front of it, he could look down onto the main floor of the garage. He saw that the drivers were grouped together, talking in whispers, near the front. Two of them had tommy-guns, and one of their number was looking out into the street through a peephole in the big rolling doors. It would be impossible to get out that way. There were at least twenty of the drivers, and there was no doubt that they were all armed. They were preparing, in case Kerrigan and Murdoch came back. It was evident that they intended to put up a fight here, if necessary, and then retreat through the secret exit over the roof.

Steve's lips were tight. He turned and went into Lemson's office and picked up the telephone. But instead of getting the outside operator, he heard the low growl of a man's voice, "What number you wanna get?"

There must be a switchboard somewhere, through which all the phones in the building cleared.

"Who's this?" the man's voice demanded. "What number do you wanna get?"

Steve smiled wryly. "Rector two-three-five-two-o," he said.

There was a second's silence, then, "What the hell! That's the F.B.I.!"

"Sure," said Steve, sharpening his voice a bit. "This is Smiley.

I got that G-man eatin' outta my hand. He's gonna make the phone call."

"Are you nuts, Smiley? You can't phone from here. The G-men will trace the call. You got to take that guy around to the cellar."

"He can't be moved," said Steve. "He'll die."

"Well, I'll connect you with the General. He's in conference, but I'll put you through. Ask him—"

"Never mind," Steve broke in hastily. "I'll wait till Marko comes back." He hung up and went out of the office. He went down the hall, and climbed the ladder up to the skylight. Then he took out one of his automatics, climbed up on to the roof.

Almost at once he saw the reason for the cunning light in Smiley's eyes when he had told about this exit.

The Realty Building abutted against the rear of the garage, and loomed four floors above it. There was a door in the high wall and a button alongside it, just as Smiley had said.

But what the thug had not mentioned, was the fact that there was a small peephole about three feet away from the door. If anyone rang that bell, there was certainly a guard who would look through the peephole. And if he saw a stranger, he would certainly shoot him down.

That must have been what Smiley counted on.

Stephen Klaw crossed the roof, stood close to the door. He touched it, and felt cold steel. It would be impossible to break it down without a torch. Almost at the same instant, he heard a grating of metal as the peephole alongside the door started to open.

Steve dropped to his stomach on the floor, hugging the wall. He heard a man inside say, "Okay, Marko. All clear."

The big steel door began to open, and Steve heard Marko's voice, "Be ready to open the door again, Pete. All the boys are coming across. The General says we got to evacuate the garage. It's no good now that Kerrigan and Murdoch know about it."

"How the hell," Pete's sharp voice demanded, "did they get wise? That cab was blown to bits."

"It gets me," Marko replied. "Those babies are devils. They can guess what's in your mind—unless Klaw came back from the dead and told them."

Marko had the door open now, and was stepping out on to the roof.

That was the moment which Stephen Klaw chose to rise up from where he was crouching.

He stuck an automatic in Marko's stomach, and grinned.

"You called it, Marko," he said cheerfully. "Here I am—back from the grave!"

Marko let out a screech, fell back. Steve Klaw came in after him.

They were in a sort of closet, probably a secret room on this floor. It was bare, except for a single chair upon which sat the man, Pete.

PETE HAD a short-muzzled shotgun under his arm. He was alert, sharp-eyed. He swung the shotgun up to cover Steve and Marko. Steve knew what he was going to do. He was going to shoot, even if he had to hit Marko as well.

Stephen Klaw didn't give him a chance to get the gun all the way up.

He gave Marko a shove, sent him hurtling into Pete. Pete pushed his chair back to get out of the way. Steve came right after Marko, with his right arm pushed out stiffly in front of him, and with the automatic gripped in his fist.

The automatic struck flush into Pete's face, smashing his nose, ripping his cheek.

Pete screamed with agony, dropped the shotgun and raised both hands to his face.

Marko recovered his balance, and clawed for a gun.

Steve grinned thinly and hit him on the side of the jaw with his left-hand automatic. Bone cracked in Marko's jaw, and the big man went down, unconscious.

Klaw swung around, reversing his automatic, and brought the butt down hard against the side of Pete's skull. Pete's scream died in his throat, and he folded over and slid off the chair alongside of Marko.

The G-man stood there for a moment, hefting his automatics, and looking down at the two badly battered and unconscious men.

"Part payment for Gregg Daly!" he murmured softly.

He turned around and closed the big steel door to the roof, then pushed home the two heavy bolts that locked it. He grinned crookedly. Those men in the garage wouldn't be able to evacuate it for a while. If Kerrigan and Murdoch did come back with a raiding party, they'd find a nice nest of rats waiting down there to be smoked out.

115

He stepped over the body of Marko, to a door in the opposite wall of the closet. It opened under his touch.

He peered out into a small room. There was a switchboard here, and a beefy-jowled man sitting in front of it, manipulating the plugs. This must be the man who had answered him when he picked up the phone in Lemson's office.

The beefy switchboard operator was facing the door through which Steve entered. He sprang up from the board and snatched a gun which had been lying close to his hand.

He swung the gun up, and Steve shot him through the heart.

The man spun backward, threw his arms in the air, and hit the wall behind him, then slid down the wall to the floor.

Steve waited, holding his breath, listening. The bark of his .32 must have been heard elsewhere on the floor. But it could very well have been mistaken for backfire.

A minute passed, and no one came in.

Steve went over to the switchboard and picked up one of the terminals and plugged it in.

"Rector two-three-five-two-o," he said to the operator.

In a moment he had the F.B.I. Field Office, and was talking to the Agent in charge. "I'm on the inside," he reported, "and getting close to the General. Where are Kerrigan and Murdoch?"

"They've taken a raiding party to the Gold Star Garage," the agent at the other end told him. "Lemson refused to talk, saying that he had pull, and would be free in an hour. But we found one of the badges of the Army of Death pinned inside his vest, so we used that as evidence to get a Federal judge to sign a search warrant. Kerrigan and Murdoch are on the way to the garage now."

"Okay," said Steve. "Better send some men to cover the block. There's a secret connection with the Realty Building, in back of the garage. I'm in here now. I think it's the third floor. Don't come in. Just cover the entrance, and stop everybody going out. Kerrigan and Murdoch and I will smoke out these rats."

He pulled out the plug, started to turn, and felt something hard jabbing into his back.

"This is a gat, mister," some one said behind him.

CHAPTER 9
SUICIDE SQUAD SHOWDOWN

"**G**LAD TO hear it!" said Steve Klaw. He swiveled on his left heel, jamming his elbow into the midsection of the man behind him. Steve felt the man's gun slide crosswise along his back, just as it exploded. The slug scorched his ribs, sending a hot lance of fire up his side.

He had put down one of his automatics when he was making the phone call. But always, from force of habit, he kept one hand in a pocket, gripping one of his automatics. He shot now, through the pocket. The slug smashed into the man's stomach.

Stephen Klaw was drenched with the blood spurting from that wound. The man gurgled hoarsely, doubled over, bleeding like a stuck pig. He fell face down on the floor, rendered unconscious by the shock of the shot fired at such close quarters.

Steve picked up his other automatic, walked around the body, and went out of the switchboard room.

What he beheld caused him to halt in amazement. He found himself in a huge office, almost half a floor in size. There were perhaps fifty desks here, all occupied by typists and stenographers, busily working at their machines. At the far end was a glassed-in row of offices where sat busy executives. Along the near wall was another row of offices, but these were not glassed-in. They boasted solid oak doors, with gold lettering.

One bore the legend, *Office of the President.* Next to it there was another door with the lettering, *Directors' Room.* Glancing across to the corridor door in the opposite wall, Steve made out the name on the glass, reading backward, *J. Augustus, Inc., Efficiency Experts.*

Many of the girls had stopped typing, and were staring at Steve's bloody clothes and scarred face. Near the door, two guards in uniform got up and started to stroll casually across the room toward him. They were wearing Sam Browne belts with holstered revolvers.

Stephen Klaw blandly disregarded them, as well as the stares of the typists. He walked over to the nearest girl's desk, and looked at what she had in the typewriter. It was circular letter to a brewery in Milwaukee, offering the services of J. Augustus, Inc., to put their business on a more efficient basis.

The girl shrank away from him.

Steve smiled down at her, and showed her his badge. "You don't have to be afraid of me, sister. But I guess your job is about over. Tell me, why do they need armed guards in a place like this?"

"B-because we handle a lot of collections for c-clients," the girl stammered.

He turned around slowly, just as the two guards came up to the desk. He pinned the badge to his coat lapel, and then thrust both hands into his pockets. He faced the guards.

"The F.B.I. is taking over here," he said tonelessly, his slate-gray eyes moving from one to the other of the two men. "Resistance will make you liable to prosecution to the full extent of the law." He started toward the door of the Directors' Room.

One of the guards stepped in his path, barring the way. He was sliding the gun out of his holster. He was a big fellow.

"I represent the United States of America," Steve said mildly. "I warn you—don't draw that gun."

The other guard already had his gun out. The one with the thick lips was just clearing the gun out of his holster.

There was no flicker of emotion in Stephen Klaw's face. He fired both automatics from his pockets.

Cauliflower-ear took the slug in his stomach. The other one got it over the heart.

Immediately pandemonium broke loose in the busy office. Girls began to shriek. Men shouted, and typewriters fell off their movable stands as the typists sprung up in panic. It was clear that all these people working in the outer office had no inkling of the sinister inside set-up of the firm by which they were employed.

Stephen Klaw stooped, picked up the revolvers of the two guards and thrust them into his breast pockets. Then, with his hands still in his outside coat pockets, he strode across the room, through the milling, panicky crowd of girls. He pushed open the door of the Directors' Room.

Twelve men stared at him from around the Directors' table. They were already on their feet, alarmed by the shooting.

Steve Klaw kicked the door shut behind him, and stood with his back to it.

"Hello, Jarger," he said. "So you're the General!"

Jarger began to laugh. His gnarled fingers were on the table. They were touching a row of buttons. "I'll make a deal with you, Klaw."

"You can't make any deal with me, Jarger. I saw what you did to Daly."

"Don't be too sure, Klaw. Do you hear that shooting? It's in the garage."

Steve Klaw had heard it. There was the quick *rat-tat-tat* of sub-machine guns, and the booming thunder of .38s.

"I hear it," said Steve. "That's my partners, Kerrigan and Murdoch. They're taking over your rats in the garage."

"Exactly, Klaw."

Jarger leaned forward over the table. For a moment his eyes nicked toward the wall at his left, where a little peephole yawned open. Steve caught that glance.

Jarger went on, "Observe where my fingers are, Klaw. I'm touching two buttons. These two buttons are wired to the same kind of bomb that was rigged in your taxicab. Only these bombs contain ten pounds each of tri-nitro-toluene. They are planted in the garage."

STEVE'S GLITTERING eyes swung around the circle of taut men who were watching him. Lou Sorgum, Jake Cadman, and the others, had not dared to move since he entered. But as they heard Jarger's confident voice, they seemed to take on new hope.

"You understand, Klaw?" asked Jarger. "That's why I ordered the garage evacuated. I knew Kerrigan and Murdoch would come back. I can blow it up now with a touch of my finger. Suppose fifteen or twenty of my own men go with it? It's worth the exchange. Kerrigan and Murdoch must have as many F.B.I. men with them."

He stopped, then added triumphantly, "You see, Klaw, a good general always has a trick in reserve. I'll trade you—the lives of your partners for the lives of everybody in this room. We walk out of here, and you guarantee that we won't be touched."

"I can't guarantee that," Steve told him tonelessly. "The building is covered. You'll be stopped."

"You needn't worry, Klaw. I have another way out of here. I have offices on the same floors in the next two buildings. The third building is the Paravox Theater on the corner. We'll slide in there, and slip out with the crowds."

"You're telling me too much," Steve said. "You wouldn't trust me to know that much."

"Of course not," Jarger said, smiling. "Part of the bargain is that you don't leave here alive. I know you and your friends. You'll gladly give up your life for Kerrigan and Murdoch, won't you?"

"Yes," said Steve Klaw. "Gladly."

"Then put your guns down on the floor."

Steve grinned. "How do I know you won't push those buttons anyway?"

Jarger threw a quick glance toward the peephole in the wall. He let out a sigh of relief, then chuckled. "I knew all along that we couldn't make a deal, Klaw. I was just stalling for time—till my bodyguard came back. Now it won't be necessary to make any deal. You are to be liquidated."

He nodded once, in a sort of signal.

Steve Klaw's eyes were on the peephole. He saw the silenced rifle poke out.

He fired six times with his left-hand gun, straight into the peephole, alongside the rifle barrel. The rifle sagged aside, and a man screamed behind that peephole, his scream almost drowned by the thunderous reverberations of Steve's guns.

His right-hand gun was spitting flame, too. Six times it barked, in perfect synchronized time with the other one. And all six slugs smashed into Augustus Jarger's chest with the force of battering-rams, hurling him back from the table, and away from the deadly row of buttons.

A roll of thunder and stench of cordite assailed ears and nose. The room shook with the din of gunfire.

The eleven men at the table were galvanized into action.

"His guns are empty!" yelled Lou Sorgum.

They all started to go for weapons.

Stephen Klaw laughed harshly. His hands darted in and out of his breast pockets, and appeared with the two revolvers he had taken from the uniformed guards. At the same time the door was violently thrust open. Steve, whose back had been to the door, was sent sprawling.

In the doorway appeared two wild and terrifying figures.

Johnny Kerrigan and Dan Murdoch, each with a tommy-gun, standing shoulder to shoulder.

Eleven men raised their hands precipitately in the air, letting their weapons clatter to the floor. Almost as if in chorus they yelled, *"Don't shoot!"*

Stephen Klaw got up from the floor, dusted his trousers.

Johnny Kerrigan heaved a sigh of relief. "I thought they got the Shrimp!"

"Hi, Shrimp!" said Dan Murdoch.

Steve Klaw grinned. "Hi, mopes!" he said. "Pretty good going—What're you gonna say?"

THE SUICIDE SQUAD'S LAST MILE

CHAPTER 1
THE SHADOW OF
MILO FLINDERS

JOHNNY KERRIGAN was driving, as usual. Dan Murdoch sat next to him. Steve Klaw was in the back, with the thin, emaciated woman. Florence Roche was her name. Her eyes were listless, and without luster. Her arms were skinny, her breasts flat, her shoulders drooping. She was trying to sit straight, and look brave. But there was a tell-tale trembling at her lips that gave her away.

"You *will* save him, won't you?" she asked Stephen Klaw. "You won't let Barney Powers take him for a ride?"

Stephen Klaw allowed no sign of sympathy to show in his slate-gray eyes.

"If what you tell us is true, Mrs. Roche, and if your husband gives us the evidence we want—we'll take care of him."

"It's true," she said tonelessly. "Mannie often told me—if he got in a jam with Barney Powers, he had the goods to spill to the F.B.I. He told me he could name the big shot that backs Barney Powers with money and influence. And today I heard it—that Mannie is slated for a one-way ride with no-return ticket. That's why I phoned your Director in Washington. I can't afford to lose

126

Back to back, the Suicide
Squad waged bitter battle!

Mannie. He's got no life insurance. In the rackets, a man can't get a policy. And I got two kids to worry about. The boy is ten, and the girl is eight." She hesitated then, and Klaw caught the gleam of a tear rolling down her rouged cheek. "And Mannie—" she said—"Mannie ain't so bad, mister. He—he's been swell!"

She stopped talking as Johnny Kerrigan swung around the corner into Desbrosses Street. Half a block away there was a sign jutting out from a two-story stucco building, wedged in between two remodeled flats. The crazily printed sign read, *Barney Powers—His Place.*

"That's it!" said Florence Roche.

Johnny Kerrigan pulled the car over to the curb. He grunted. "Like all these village joints. They think it's smart to write their signs like that."

"That sign isn't the only screwy thing about Barney Powers' place," Florence Roche said bitterly. "It's the worst clip joint in the city. An honest man's life isn't worth a dime in there. I know. I used to work there—before I married Mannie and lost my looks."

Stephen Klaw patted her hand. "Take it easy, Mrs. Roche. We'll get Mannie out of there for you—provided you've been on the level with us."

He got out of the car. Dan Murdoch got out, too.

Suddenly, the strain became too much for Florence Roche. She began to sob quietly. She gulped hard, and wiped her eyes.

"I'm afraid, Mr. Klaw," she said through the window, "I'm afraid it's no good. Maybe I'm sending you to your death."

Steve gave her a crooked smile. "That's what we're paid for."

"I know, I know," she said. "You three are the F.B.I.'s Suicide Squad. They only give you the hopeless assignments. Everybody in the rackets knows about you three—Kerrigan and Murdoch and Klaw. That's why I'm afraid. They'll kill you on sight the minute you set foot in Barney Powers' place."

Stephen Klaw didn't answer her. He nodded to Dan Murdoch, and started down the street, his hands dug deep in his coat pockets.

"So long, Mopes," he said to Kerrigan and Murdoch.

"So long, Shrimp," they chorused. And then Murdoch added, "Watch yourself, Shrimp. I'll be right outside. One shot—and I come after you!"

Steve Klaw nodded, and kept on walking. Murdoch followed, about fifty feet behind.

Klaw turned in at the entrance of Barney Powers' place, still keeping his hands deep in his pockets. A huge doorman, dressed like an 1890 policeman, attempted to stop him. He got squarely in the way and swung his short nightstick.

"Wait a minute, mister. Where you going?"

"Inside," said Steve. "This is a public place—or am I wrong?"

"It's a public place, all right. But the tables is all taken." His jaw was squared.

"All right. I'll stand at the bar."

Steve started to push past, but the doorman put a huge paw against his chest. "Sorry. The bar is closed—"

Stephen Klaw took his right hand out of his pocket. It was holding a black automatic.

The doorman gulped, and stopped talking.

Steve grinned. "Get the idea?"

"You're crazy, mister. This is Barney Powers' Place. If you're aiming to start trouble—"

"That's just what I'm aiming to do, my friend." Steve moved around behind the doorman and gave him a shove. He went sprawling, and landed in Dan Murdoch's arms. Dan Murdoch gave him a quick frisk, found a gun in a shoulder holster. Before the man could open his mouth to protest, Dan had the handcuffs on him, and was propelling him back to the car at the corner.

Stephen Klaw didn't wait to see what happened. He put his hand back in his pocket, and entered. He brushed past the hat-check girl without surrendering his hat, and stopped just inside the dining-room.

A GIRL on the stage was doing a strip-tease number under a spotlight. The tables were all taken, mostly by flashy men and provocatively dressed girls. The bar was at one side, and seven or eight men who were lined up there, suddenly stopped drinking and stared at Stephen Klaw.

Klaw paid them no attention. His glance swung around the dining-room, and came to rest upon one of the tables along the wall.

Three men were sitting at that table. Two of them had their hands out of sight. The third had his hands in plain view. He was nervously rolling an empty beer glass between them. He was sweating a little, and his collar was wilted. The third man was Mannie Roche. He was very scared.

Stephen Klaw headed for that table.

Mannie Roche saw him first, and grew tense. A quick look of

hope flitted across his thin and frightened face, but as quickly disappeared.

The two other men at the table frowned when Steve Klaw stopped, facing them. He kept his hands in his pockets, and his eyes on the two men, though he spoke to Mannie Roche.

"Hello, Roche," he said. "Know me?"

"Yes," said Roche, wetting his lips. "I know you."

"Your wife sent me," Steve said. "To talk to you."

The two men at the table with Roche scowled. The one at Mannie's left was squat, with heavy black eyebrows. It was he who spoke.

"Scram, mister," he growled. "Mannie has important business with us."

Stephen Klaw raised his eyebrows. "How about introducing me to your friends, Mannie?"

Roche wiped perspiration from his forehead. "This—this is Gus Skarff—" indicating the squat one. "And this is Sudsy Fiorio."

Steve grinned. "A couple of prime killers, eh? Were you boys thinking of taking a walk? I've got something to talk to Mannie about—in private."

Gus Skarff's face grew red. "Look here, Klaw, we know you. But you can't bluff us. You got a rep—'Killer' Klaw they call you. Well, you don't rate around here. You try something—"

"Glad to oblige," said Steve.

He came around the table toward Skarff.

Skarff brought his hand up from under the table. It had a gun in it.

But before he could raise the gun, Steve Klaw hit him in the jaw.

Klaw was built slim and wiry. He might almost have been taken for a kid. But that right of his connected like a battering-ram. Gus Skarff went over backward, chair and all. The sudden racket sent a hush through the place. The orchestra broke off in the middle of a note. The strip-tease girl stopped like a frozen image, with one band of her brassiere undone, and the curve of her white breast showing above it.

Gus Skarff glared murderously up at Steve from his awkward position on the floor. He still had a grip on his gun, which he lifted up.

Klaw stepped in lithely and brought a heel down on Skarff's hand. Skarff yelled with the pain of crushed bones, and let go the gun. Steve kicked it under the table. He turned and faced the bar.

The men there had begun to move forward in a body, their hands hovering at their shoulders. Klaw grinned at them mirthlessly. He had both of his hands back in his coat pockets. He said nothing, just stared at them.

Abruptly, they wavered. Someone muttered, "It's Killer Klaw. The rest of the Suicide Squad must be around!"

"He's got a gun in each pocket," someone else said hoarsely. "He never misses!"

The men began to shuffle back to the bar.

Stephen Klaw shrugged, almost disappointedly. He looked over to Sudsy Fiorio, the other man at the table.

"Scram," he said.

Fiorio's face was white. He got up and backed away across the room, bumping into tables until he reached the bar.

Gus Skarff got to his feet, cursing under his breath, and nursing his crushed hand. He turned and slunk away, disappearing through a door at the rear. The orchestra began to play again. The girl resumed her strip-tease number, but her heart wasn't in it any more.

Steve Klaw, still smiling that cold, hard smile of his, pulled a chair around and sat down opposite Mannie Roche—in such a way that he commanded a view of the bar as well as of the rear door. He was set.

"Okay, Roche," he said. "Talk. Your wife claims you have something the F.B.I. can use. If that's true, I'll take you out of here alive."

Roche shivered. "It can't be done, Mister Klaw. Those gorillas at the bar are only waiting for you to make a move. And Barney Powers has more men in the back. Skarff and Fiorio were holding me here till Barney Powers comes back with a car. They as much as told me I was going for a ride."

Steve Klaw shrugged. "Okay, Roche. If you don't want to try—"

"Wait! Don't go, for God's sake. Listen, Mister Klaw, I can give you the name of the guy behind Powers."

"I know his name," Steve said. "What I want is evidence—evidence that we can arrest him on."

"I can give you that," said the other. "Milo Flinders is the big shot. He's got an office in Washington, and everybody thinks he's a respectable business man. He sends out a market letter on the stock market every day. But that's only a cover. His real business is financing guys like Barney Powers all over the country."

"I know all that, Roche," Steve said. "But there's no proof yet."

Roche was talking out of the side of his mouth. He, too, was watching the bar and the rear door. He was fumbling in his vest pocket, and suddenly Steve felt something being pushed into his hand under the table.

"Take it, Klaw, quick!"

Steve did not look down. By the sense of touch he knew that the object which Roche had given him was a small pasteboard square.

"It's a parcel check, Mister Klaw. Pennsylvania Station. A brief-case. The evidence you want is in that brief-case. Two weeks ago, Barney Powers needed ten grand quick. He sent me to Washington to get the dough from Milo Flinders. I held out one of the grand notes—told Barney I'd lost it. That's why I'm on the spot now."

Steve's face showed nothing. "How can that grand note convict Milo Flinders?"

"It's hot money, Mister Klaw," said the other. "I checked the serial numbers. It comes from that Brooklyn bank robbery a year ago. Flinders was holding it till it cooled off, but when Powers called for dough he had to use it. And it has Milo Flinders' fingerprints on it. I dropped one of the notes, and he picked it up."

"I see," Steve Klaw said softly. "All right, Roche. I'll take you out of here. And I'll see that you have protection till Flinders is convicted."

Roche shook his head sadly. "I don't expect to get out of here alive any more, Mister Klaw. I'm only telling you this because I want my wife and kids to get a break. I don't want them to get it like Jake Lampson's family. Remember them, Mister Klaw?"

Roche's eyes reflected the horror of what he was thinking. "Remember? Lampson tried to squeal on the big shot. There was some talk that he could name Milo Flinders. So what happened? The local cops gave him protection. And Flinders sent a gang in and they took over the whole damned apartment-house where Lampson lived. They ran it. Nobody suspected what was happening inside—till they found Lampson and his wife and kids, tortured to death!"

"I remember," said Stephen Klaw. "I remember very well. That's why we're trying to get Flinders—to stop things like that. I'll protect you, Roche. You have my word."

Mannie Roche shook his head again. There was a queer, hopeless quirk to his lips. "It can't be done, Mister Klaw. I ain't expecting anything for myself. You go away with that check, and turn in the evidence. Leave me here. I'll take my medicine. They'd never let me leave—"

"I promised your wife I'd take you out of here," Klaw said grimly. "And that's what I'm going to do!"

CHAPTER 2
"I WANT YOUR EARS!"

K LAW PUSHED back his chair, and rose. "Get up!" he ordered. Roche arose. He looked beaten and hopeless.

"There's not a chance, Mister Klaw. Look at those guys. They're ganging at the door."

Sudsy Fiorio and the other men at the bar had moved over slowly till they were at the front end of the bar. Three of them had edged around behind the bar. It was clear that they weren't going to let anyone get out that door. They figured that Roche had made his deal with the F.B.I.

Just then the rear door opened violently, and a big, bald-headed man appeared there. Behind him, Steve saw the faces of half a dozen others. The big bald-headed man came slowly into the dining-room, ignoring the people at the tables, the strip-tease girl on the stage—ignoring everybody but Stephen Klaw. He stopped just alongside the bar.

Mannie Roche, shivering alongside Steve Klaw, whispered, "It's Barney Powers! Gawd, he'll never let us get out of here."

Klaw had his hands in his pockets. "Follow me!" he said out of the corner of his mouth, and started for the door.

He saw Barney Powers motion with his hand to the orchestra leader, who waved his baton. The orchestra struck up a crashing, resounding march tune, which filled the room with sound—enough sound, Steve noted grimly, to almost drown out the noise of gunfire.

At the same time Barney Powers nodded to the men at the front of the bar. Guns appeared in their hands. The men from the rear came streaming into the room past Powers, also producing guns.

Powers watched everything at once, grinning with insolent confidence. This act had evidently been well rehearsed. No doubt it had been performed often in the past. On many occasions, men had been known to go into Barney Powers' place, and never come out again—on their own steam. And no one ever talked about what happened when the music began to crash—because no one wanted a dose of the same thing for himself.

The strip-tease girl must have seen this act before—must have known what was going to happen. For she faltered in her last step, as she was backing out into the wings, with only a thin scarf between her nakedness and the eyes of the audience. The swift change in the rhythm of the music might have accounted for her faltering... but not for the desperate speed with which she ran off the stage.

Stephen Klaw became motionless, in the center of the room. Mannie Roche clung closely to his side.

Klaw's cold, slate-gray eyes were narrowed now, almost to slits. His lips were tight and thin. Anyone who had ever in the past mistaken him for just a kid, would recognize his error now.

Perhaps those thugs saw that thing in him which had always frightened his enemies. Surely, they had seen it a few minutes ago when they back-watered. But now it was different. Their boss, Barney Powers, was watching and in command. Besides, they had reinforcements. Those men who had come in with Powers were at the other end of the room, also with guns in their hands. Klaw could not move backward or forward without meeting an enemy. They could enfilade him, whichever direction he took to retreat.

The one thing they didn't expect was that Stephen Klaw would *not* retreat.

His motions in response to this new development were as swift as the speed of instinctive reaction. Instinct, as a characteristic of the born fighting man, is a surer thing than reason or plan. Another man might have reasoned that since the front and rear were covered, it would be good strategy to stand and fight. Stephen Klaw reached the same decision by instinct, in one twentieth of the time.

Almost before those men at the bar had finished disposing themselves in front of the door, Klaw acted.

He reached out with his left hand and seized the end of the nearest table, which had already been deserted by its occupants. He up-ended the table, and shoved Mannie Roche down under its protection.

"Stay behind that!" he ordered.

Then his hand slid back into the coat pocket. It emerged, at the same time as his right. In each fist was a black automatic.

Sudsy Fiorio, at the head of the men near the front, was snarling, vindictive. He was eager to wipe out the shame of his retreat a few minutes ago. He looked across at Barney Powers, who nodded.

"Take them, boys!" Powers yelled, above the crashing sound of the music.

SUDSY FIORIO fired first. Then the others began to trigger their guns. Gunfire crashed through the chords of music to make a terrible, deafening cacophony of discordant thunder. Lead whined past Stephen Klaw from two directions.

He did not duck, or move back. He stood spraddle-legged in the center of the room with that fixed smile upon his face, and the hard cold gleam in his slate-gray eyes. His body did not move an inch. Only his hands. They jumped with each recoil of his .32 caliber automatics.

He fired them in unison—*one, two—one, two—one, two*— like a master musician handling instruments he loved. And he made those weapons sing. The right-hand gun toward the front, the left-hand gun toward the rear. He seemed to be looking and shooting in both directions at once.

Men fell at the front and at the rear. Yet the slim and wiry figure of Stephen Klaw seemed impervious to lead. Those gunmen were shooting quickly, frantically—perhaps a little wildly. They had heard many stories about the Suicide Squad. They had heard how Kerrigan and Murdoch and Klaw always seemed to go *looking* for death—and yet had never, so far, found it. They had heard how Kerrigan and Murdoch and Klaw had taken whole gangs in their stride. They had never heard of a man who faced their guns and lived to tell it. Maybe it was that psychological factor which made them shoot a little too quickly, a bit too feverishly—in the effort to cut him down before he could get them.

In the first thirty seconds of that mad inferno of thunderous gunfire and crashing music, Klaw had the psychological edge on his side. After that, he had much more material help. For two terrible and formidable figures appeared in the entrance from the hat-check hall.

They were Kerrigan and Murdoch....

Shoulder to shoulder they stood there, like two avenging gods out of some fantastic warrior's heaven, with a gun in each fist.

The huge, powerful Johnny Kerrigan, and the tall, handsome, dark-haired Dan Murdoch. Only a single glance each of them spared, to make sure that Stephen Klaw was still on his feet. And then their guns joined the music.

That did the trick. The gunmen were seized with a sudden terrible panic as lead from six mercilessly accurate guns blasted into them.

"It's the whole damned Suicide Squad!" someone screamed.

And then, a stream of desperate, frantic, fear-stricken men trod upon each other in a wild stampede toward the rear door. The music trailed off into silence, as the shooting ended. The musicians sat limp and frightened in the pit, knowing that they would never be paid off for this night's work.

Kerrigan and Murdoch and Klaw stopped shooting. Steve Klaw lowered his guns and looked around for Barney Powers. But the owner of the place had ducked out when the fracas began. He was nowhere in sight.

Johnny Kerrigan and Dan Murdoch came into the room, grinning. They did not attempt to pursue the fleeing gunmen. Johnny Kerrigan raised his voice to reassure the patrons.

"It's all right, people!" he called. "Take it easy, and no one will be hurt."

He patted Steve Klaw on the back. "Glad to see you're all in one piece, Shrimp!"

Steve said, "Nice shooting, Mopes. You didn't come any too soon."

He bent and helped Mannie Roche to his feet. Mannie was

unhurt, but his shirt was wringing wet with perspiration, and his collar was entirely wilted.

"God!" he exclaimed. "I never thought you could do it!"

By that time the police had appeared on the scene.

STEVE KLAW led Mannie Roche out into the street and back to the car where his wife was waiting, while Kerrigan and Murdoch talked to the detectives. In a few minutes they came out and joined him at the car.

Steve gave them the baggage check. "Roche here, says the evidence is in his brief-case. A thousand-dollar bill that will hang Milo Flinders."

Johnny Kerrigan whistled. "Nice stuff—if it's true!"

"You and Dan get that brief-case and take it to Washington by the next train," Steve told them swiftly.

"What about you, Shrimp?" Johnny asked.

Steve nodded toward the white faces of Mannie and Florence Roche, in the car. "I promised to protect them. I'm taking them home—and staying with them. Barney Powers is free—and dangerous."

Kerrigan nodded. "Okay, Shrimp. But watch yourself. Remember, we won't be around to pull you out of a hot-spot—"

He just barely ducked a haymaker that Steve swung at him, and danced away, grinning.

Just then the police sergeant in charge came over. "Sorry to hold you up," he said. "But I got to ask a few routine questions. It'll only take a few minutes. Looks like Barney Powers and some of his mob got away. But we'll round them up all right."

The routine questions took almost twenty minutes. Florence and Mannie Roche waited in the car....

But there was one person who did not stay. A short, ferret-faced individual had been loitering near the curb, and had overheard the conversation of the three G-men. This individual, without attracting attention, now managed to remove himself from the crowd. Once out of sight, he hurried his pace until he reached the corner drugstore. Eagerly, he wedged himself into a booth, dialed a number. Then he glued his mouth to the phone, and spoke rapidly.

"Boss! This is Pim," he said. "I was watching outside of Powers' place like you told me. Kerrigan and Murdoch and Klaw came, with the Roche dame, like you figured. Klaw went in alone. But Powers' mob couldn't take him. They got Roche out, and the whole damned three of that Suicide Squad is still alive. They got the evidence, too. Kerrigan and Murdoch is taking the eleven o'clock train to Washington, and Klaw is gonna take Roche and his wife up to their house."

At the other end of that telephone line, a tall thin man with a hawk-like face, topped by pure white hair, listened carefully to every word which Pim uttered. At the end of the report he said softly, "All right, Pim. I didn't expect that Powers would be able to take those three hellions. Now I'll use my own plan. Did Powers get away?"

"Yes, Boss. I guess he's gone to the other hideout."

"Very well," said the other man. "Go there at once. Tell him to take every available man he has up to Riverdale where Roche lives. I'll meet him there, and bring more men of my own. Tell him to hurry. We must have everything set before Klaw gets up there!"

"But what about Kerrigan and Murdoch, Boss? They'll be on the way to Washington with the evidence—"

"No they won't, Pim—not when I've got this thing arranged. Pim, this is going to be the Suicide Squad's last mile!"

Milo Flinders hung up, and gently stroked his white hair with a long and aristocratic hand. There was a gentle smile upon his lips, which belied the terrible look of hate in his vulture-eyes. He had flown from Washington expressly to oversee the efforts of Barney Powers to prevent the Suicide Squad from getting Roche's evidence. Now he was taking charge personally.

To look at Milo Flinders, one would have taken him for a political lobbyist, or perhaps, even a senator or congressman. He had the carriage and poise of dignified authority. Only the F.B.I. suspected that he was the true head of as vicious a combine of underworld racketeers as had ever committed crimes, from arson to murder, in most large cities of the nation. And the F.B.I. would never be able to put the finger on him if Kerrigan and Murdoch didn't get to Washington.

"Yes," Milo Flinders murmured softly. "I shall have to oversee this myself. This *must* be the Suicide Squad's Last Mile!"

His gentle affectation fell away from him. He pressed a button, and a man appeared in the doorway. Staccato, rapid-fire instructions issued from his lips. Now he was displaying the deadly shrewdness and cunning which had placed him in his position of secret underworld power....

SO WHEN, at the end of a half hour of police routine and

red tape, Stephen Klaw finally managed to get into the F.B.I. car with Mannie and Florence Roche, he was unaware that he was setting out upon what had been planned as his 'last mile.'

Kerrigan and Murdoch left in a cab for Pennsylvania Station, where they were to pick up the brief-case containing the evidence. They had ample time to spare before making the eleven o'clock train, but they wanted to get their hands on the brief-case at once.

Steve Klaw watched them go, then headed the F.B.I. car north, toward Riverdale, where Mannie Roche lived.

Florence was quietly sobbing in her husband's arms in the back. "I never thought I'd see you alive again, Mannie."

"I don't care about myself any more," he told her. "It's you and the kids, Flo. I'm afraid of what Barney Powers will do to you."

She looked with confidence at the wiry back of Stephen Klaw. Her eyes were shining. *"He'll* take care of us!" She pressed her husband's hand against her breast. "You've got to go straight from now on, Mannie. Quit the rackets. Get a job—any kind of job—so our kids can be proud of their father!"

"I'll do it!" Mannie Roche breathed. "So help me, I'll do it!"

"If you mean that," Steve Klaw said over his shoulder, "I'll see if I can get you something. You'll have to testify at Milo Flinders' trial, of course. After that, maybe I can help you get a job." He said it gruffly, but they sensed the sympathy beneath his hard manner.

They were up in Riverdale now, high up above the level of the city, with a steep drop to the Hudson, and a magnificent view of the Jersey shore. There were no buildings here, except for one apartment house about a quarter of a mile away.

"That's where I live," Mannie said. "Barney Powers owns the house. He lets me live rent free while I work for him." Roche shivered. "I should've moved out long ago. This neighborhood is too lonely. You could do fifty murders here, and no one would know it!"

"What's that construction shack up there?" Steve asked, pointing to a shanty up on a hill off the road, where there seemed to be some building going on.

"That's another apartment house that Barney Powers is putting up," Mannie said. "He owns a lot of land around here, but it really belongs to Milo Flinders. It's just in Barney's name."

"I see," said Stephen Klaw. The shack was about a thousand feet from the apartment house, which was a ten-story structure, boasting the name, *Shore-crest Apartments.*

Steve swung into the parking lot alongside the building, and got out of the car.

"I'm going up with you," he said. "I'll stay here till the Field Office sends over a couple of men. You'll be guarded night and day till you go to Washington to testify."

They went up to the sixth floor in the self-service elevator.

On the way up, Mannie Roche said, "Gawd, I'm beginning to get the jitters. I was thinking of Lucy Fenstone, who tried to run out on Milo Flinders last year. She used to handle his books."

"I remember her," Steve said.

"Remember how her brother disappeared, and she got a package with the kid's ears?" Mannie groaned. "She closed up like a clam after that. The kid was never found. That's a favorite trick of Flinders'—cutting off a guy's ears for a souvenir. Everybody knows these things, but no one can prove them."

"Maybe this is the end!" Florence Roche whispered. "Maybe Mannie will be the instrument of bringing Milo Flinders to justice!"

They got off at the sixth floor. Mannie inserted the key in the door, and opened it as quietly as possible.

"Ronnie and May will be sound asleep now," he explained. "Don't want to wake them up."

Stephen Klaw went in close behind him. The living-room was in darkness. Steve felt a queer sense of danger as he heard Mannie Roche fumbling for the electric light switch. Instinctively, his hands dug down into his coat pockets.

And then the lights went on.

Florence Roche uttered a strangled little cry. Mannie said, "God, no!"

Stephen Klaw stood still, with his hands in his pockets, staring with narrowed eyes at what he saw across the room....

BARNEY POWERS was there, with Sudsy Fiorio and another thug. They had lined up a couch and an upholstered armchair as a sort of barricade. They were behind that barricade. In front of it stood two frightened little children, in pyjamas—a boy of ten, and a girl of about eight.

Sudsy Fiorio had hold of the girl's hair from behind, and the other thug was reaching out one arm from behind the couch to hold onto the little boy's throat. With their free hands they were pointing guns at the backs of the children's heads.

Bald-headed Barney Powers was standing farther down, behind the armchair, with a revolver trained on Steve Klaw. He was grinning wickedly.

"We figured you right, Mister G-man!" he said. "We figured you'd come here to protect this rat and his family!"

Florence Roche started forward toward her children, but Powers' revolver waved her back.

"For God's sake," she choked, "don't harm them. They never did anything!"

Powers laughed. "It's up to Klaw whether these kids get hurt—or not!"

Steve Klaw did not move. "What do you want, Powers?" he asked tonelessly.

Barney Powers laughed. "I knew you'd listen to reason, Klaw. We want you, and that rat, Mannie. Take out your guns, Klaw. Take them out very carefully, and put them down on the floor. If you make a bad move, we'll let these two kids have it."

"God!" whispered Mannie Roche.

"They'll kill me. But I don't care—if they only let the kids go."

Steve's gray eyes met those of Barney Powers across the room. "You wouldn't dare to hurt those kids," he said. "You'd be lynched."

Barney Powers grinned. "I'm not fooling, Klaw. There'll be a warrant out for us anyway. Two kids more won't make any difference. I want your ears, Klaw. The ears of Killer Klaw. And then I'll get those two pals of yours—Kerrigan and Murdoch. Do you think I'd let two kids stand in the way?"

"Even a rat like you wouldn't kill children, Powers."

Barney Powers shrugged. "Okay, Klaw. Here they go!" He jerked his head toward Fiorio and the other thug. "Give it to them, Sudsy!"

"Wait!" said Steve Klaw hoarsely. His face showed no sign of emotion, except for a little muscle in his cheek, which twitched spasmodically. "You win!" he said very quietly.

Slowly and carefully he took the two automatics out of his pocket and laid them on the floor....

CHAPTER III
TWO TICKETS TO DEATH

JOHNNY KERRIGAN was pretty happy. But Dan Murdoch looked glum. They were in Pennsylvania Station, in front of Track Eleven. The Washington Express was scheduled to leave in twenty minutes, and they were waiting for the gate to open. Kerrigan had a brief-case under his arm. They had gotten it in exchange for the baggage check, and Johnny had opened it and seen the thousand-dollar note in an envelope, inside.

"What are you looking sour about?" he asked Murdoch. "We came into town two hours ago, and knocked off a nice piece of work. All we have to do is take this to Washington, and get a warrant for Milo Flinders. Then we go on leave. From your long face, anybody would think we'd flopped!"

"That's the trouble," said Dan Murdoch. "It's gone off too easy. I have a feeling that something is wrong. Those two ginzos over near the information booth have been keeping an eye on us ever since we got here."

Johnny Kerrigan looked hopeful. "Maybe they'll try to stop us—"

He was interrupted by the sound of his name being paged through the station. It was a Western Union boy. He was coming toward the gate and calling, *"Mister* Kerrigan! *Mister* Murdoch!"

Johnny motioned to the boy, who came over to them. He said, "You gentlemen named Kerrigan and Murdoch?"

Dan nodded, and the boy handed him a package.

Johnny Kerrigan kept his eyes on the two men near the information booth. The boy waited while Murdoch opened the package. He unwrapped the brown wrapping paper, exposing a shoebox. He lifted the lid a little way, and looked inside. Then he quickly closed the lid. He turned the box over, and saw that there was a message crudely printed on the bottom, with black crayon. He read it through swiftly, and then looked up at the messenger boy. His face was bleak.

"Where did you get this package, boy?" he asked.

"Up in Riverdale, mister. The call came to go to the Shore-crest Apartments, and a man met me in front of the house and gave me the box."

"What did this man look like?"

"He was big, and kind of square-faced," said the messenger. "He took off his hat to mop the sweat for a minute, and I saw that he was bald."

Dan Murdoch's eyes flickered. "Listen to me, boy. We're agents of the F.B.I. I want you to go back to your office and wait there for us. Don't go out on any more calls. Do you understand?"

"Y-yes, sir." The boy took a look at the identification card which Murdoch showed him, and nodded. "Okay, Mister Murdoch."

Dan got the exact location where the boy had received the package, then sent him away. Now he looked at Kerrigan, who was watching him curiously.

"What's in that box, Dan?"

"Follow me, Johnny!"

Murdoch led the way swiftly across the station to the men's room. As soon as they got inside, he opened the box again and showed the contents to Johnny. They were a pair of human ears—freshly severed, with the blood dripping from the ends.

Johnny Kerrigan started to say something, then suddenly shut his lips tight. He watched as Murdoch turned the box around, and let him read the message:

> Kerrigan and Murdoch:
>
> These are the ears of your pal, Killer Klaw. We'll get your ears too, if you take the Washington train. We have enough men to stop you before you get to Washington. Be wise. Check that brief-case again, and be ready to hand over the check—or else.

There was no signature.

Johnny Kerrigan muttered a low-voiced oath. He took another look in the box. "Hell! Those are just the size of Steve's ears. But I don't believe it. Steve would never let anyone get his—ears!"

"He would," Dan Murdoch said slowly, "if he were dead!"

Johnny Kerrigan drew in his breath. "What are we waiting for then? Let's go and find out—"

Murdoch put a hand on his arm. "That's just what Powers wants us to do. He made sure the messenger boy would be able to describe him for us. And he knows we know that Roche lives in Riverdale. He expects us to come looking for Steve."

"It's a trap, then!"

Dan nodded. "Right."

"Okay," said Kerrigan. "Let's walk into his damn trap!"

"The minute we walk out of the station," Murdoch said thoughtfully, "those two ginzos who've been tailing us will phone him. He'll know we're on the way. And remember this brief-case. It has to get to Washington."

"To hell with the brief-case!" Kerrigan growled. "We got to find out about the Shrimp!"

"Okay," said Murdoch. He wrapped up the shoebox, and they stuck it in the brief-case. Then they went out of the men's room.

Just outside the door, they saw the two men who had been tailing them. Murdoch's eyes sparkled with a sudden idea. "Let's take these two guys first, Johnny!"

"And how!" said Kerrigan.

They walked directly toward the two men.

Murdoch smiled at them pleasantly. "Were you gentlemen by any chance following us?"

The two thugs were a little taken aback. Both were husky-looking gorillas—both bulging at the left shoulders. One wore a green-checked suit, the other a blue pin-stripe, with tie and shirt to match.

Pin-stripe grinned. "Following you? Perish the thought, mister. We was just waiting for a street-car!"

Murdoch's eyes were bleak. "Turn around," he said harshly, "and walk over toward Track Eleven!"

Green-check got ugly. "Says who? You G-guys think you can boss everybody around? We got as much right in this station as you!"

"So!" said Murdoch. "You know we're G-men!"

"What about it? We ain't going no place. We're staying right here!"

"You're mistaken, my friend. If you'll take the trouble to look, you'll see that's a gun that Mr. Kerrigan is holding under the brief-case."

Both looked; their eyes widened. "You—you wouldn't use that cannon in here—"

"That's what you think," Johnny Kerrigan told him with a tight grin. He hefted the brief-case under his left arm. "We got Steve Klaw's ears in a shoebox. Just give me an excuse to sink some lead in your guts, my friend!"

PIN-STRIPE LOOKED at Green-check, and Green-check looked back at Pin-stripe. Both their faces were a little greenish. They saw the savage glint in Johnny Kerrigan's eyes. Slowly they turned around and started to walk toward Track Eleven.

Johnny Kerrigan moved over to one side of them, Dan Murdoch to the other. At the gate, Murdoch nodded to the conductor, who let them through with a smile and nod. He knew them both, because they had traveled hundreds of times on this train, on their government passes. He automatically tabbed them as returning to Washington with two prisoners.

"Take Compartment A in Car Fourteen, Mr. Murdoch," he said. "Where's your friend—Mr. Klaw?"

"I wish I knew," said Murdoch.

He and Kerrigan herded their two prisoners down the platform to Car 14. The porter at the door greeted them.

"Good evenin', Mister Kerrigan. Good evenin', Mr. Murdoch. Wheah's yo' pa'tner—Mister Stevie?"

"Ask me later, Sam," Kerrigan said gloomily.

They pushed their two prisoners along the corridor to Compartment A, and thrust them through the door.

Pin-stripe exclaimed, "Hey! What the hell! This ain't constitutional! A man's got his rights. You can't arrest us like this, without no warrant—"

"We aren't exactly arresting you, my friend," Dan Murdoch said softly. He stepped up close to Pin-stripe, and brought his bunched fist up in a short arc to the man's jaw. Pin-stripe's head snapped back like a marionette's, and he fell sideways on the seat.

Green-check's hand darted to the gun in his shoulder holster, but he never got it out, because Johnny Kerrigan's ham-like fist smacked into his jaw like a ten-ton sledgehammer. He collapsed on top of Pin-stripe.

Kerrigan massaged his knuckles. "What next, Dan?"

Swiftly, Murdoch explained his plan. Johnny's eyes glistened. They went to work. In five minutes the two thugs, still dead to the world, were securely gagged and bound. Murdoch and Kerrigan used the towels from the lavatory to tie them, then soaked the towels in water so they wouldn't come undone easily. They laid the two bound men on the two bunks, face down, and put their hats on, then threw a sheet over each, leaving the upper part of their heads exposed. Into the hatband of each of them, the G-men put the government railroad passes on which they themselves traveled. Then they stood back and surveyed their work with genuine satisfaction.

To anyone looking into the compartment, it would seem that the two occupants were taking a nap—maybe a little unconventionally, with their hats on. To make it look more plausible, Murdoch took a whiskey flask which he found in Pin-stripe's pocket, and laid it on the floor.

"That does it," he said. "If Barney Powers has spies planted on this train, they'll have every reason to believe that those two muggs are Kerrigan and Murdoch—sleeping off a drunk!"

Johnny nodded. "Okay, let's go. The train pulls out in two minutes. We don't want to stay on it. We've got to find out what happened to Steve!"

They turned to go out of the compartment, stopped short. Sam, the colored porter, was in the doorway, goggling wide-eyed.

Murdoch leaped across and seized him by the wrist.

"Sam! How much did you see?"

The porter's eyes rolled. "I—I seen *ever'thing*, Mister Dan. I seen you tie them up—" he gulped, then suddenly grinned. "But you don't have to worry about me talking. I admire to be a G-man myself some day. I been taking a correspondence course. I wouldn't talk, Mister Dan. Anything you and Mister Johnny does is okay with me!"

Murdoch grinned. "Good boy, Sam." Suddenly he snapped his fingers. He gripped the lapels of the porter's white coat. "Do you really want to do something for the F.B.I.?"

"*Do* I? Try me!"

Murdoch thrust the shoebox at him. "Then here's your chance. This box contains evidence which must be delivered in Washington. It's practically the same as dynamite, if certain persons learn you've got it. Kerrigan and I can't take it. We—er—have other business here in town. Now—" he looked solemn—"can we depend on *you* to deliver this personally to our Director in Washington?"

Sam took the box almost reverently. "Mister Dan, you can depend on me. I'll deliver this box—if it costs me my life!"

"Good boy, Sam. And don't say a word about these two ginzos to the conductor. If anyone should ask you about us, say that the two guys in Compartment A are sleeping off a drunk. That's all!"

"Thanks, Mister Dan," Sam said fervently. "I appreciate this chance!"

When Kerrigan and Murdoch left him in the vestibule, his eyes were shining with a holy light. They swung off the train farther down toward the dining-car, just as the last bell rang. They watched the cars pull out of the terminal. Then they made their way to the street by the baggage exit, in case Powers had any more spies watching.

Once in the street, they hopped a cab. "Straight up to Riverdale!" Kerrigan snapped. Then to Murdoch, "By God, Dan, if the Shrimp is dead, I'm going to get hold of Barney Powers and squeeze his neck until he's stiff!"

CHAPTER 4
THE EARS OF STEPHEN KLAW

WHEN STEPHEN KLAW put his guns down on the floor at the command of Barney Powers, there was a bitter taste in his mouth. He had pledged himself to protect Mannie Roche. But he knew very well that neither he nor Mannie was scheduled to leave this house alive.

Sudsy Fiorio and the other thug—whose name was Jake Miklis—kept their grips on the two frightened children. Barney Powers came out from behind the couch. He picked up Steve Klaw's guns, pocketed them, all the while keeping his own revolver moving in an arc to cover Mannie, Flo, and Steve. His eyes glowed with satisfaction.

"There's gonna be a great time in the old town tonight," he grinned, "when the news goes out that the whole damned Suicide Squad has got the ax!"

"What do you mean—the *whole* Suicide Squad?" Steve Klaw demanded, with suddenly narrowing eyes.

"Just watch and see, sucker!"

Powers backed across the room to the telephone. He picked it up and dialed a number. In a moment he got his connection. He winked to Fiorio and Miklis, who kept their grips on the boy and girl, then spoke into the instrument.

"Boss? This is Barney," he said. "Everything is okay. We got the little guy. He quit cold when he saw it was him or the kids. I got the mob coming up. We'll take charge of the building, like you planned. Then we'll send the ears to Kerrigan and Murdoch before they make the train. I'll get the sawbones. He's waiting in a car in the back alley."

He hung up, and went over to the kitchen door, which he pushed open. His gun swung around toward Steve.

"In here, sucker!"

Stephen Klaw threw a quick glance at Mannie and Flo. Florence Roche had eyes only for her two children. It was evident that she was aching to throw herself forward against the guns of Fiorio and Miklis, and try to save them. But there wasn't a chance. The children would be dead before she reached the other side of the room.

Mannie Roche looked at Steve. "It's tough, Mister Klaw," he whispered. "Tough to die. But I can take it—as long as it's for the kids."

"I can take it too, Mannie," Steve said, "But I feel like a heel. I got you into this."

Powers waved impatiently with the gun, and Steve shrugged, and crossed the room. He went through into the kitchen and his lips thinned at what he saw there. A cot had been set up in the middle of the kitchen. Several lengths of rope, and a couple of sheets were lying beside it. Two husky gorillas with drawn guns were waiting.

Powers grinned. "This is Killer Klaw, boys—the holy terror of the Suicide Squad. Look how easy it was to take him. Believe me, after we get his ears, everybody in the rackets will have respect for our boss. We'll be sitting on top of the world!"

He turned to Steve and said ironically. "Meet two of the boys, Klaw—Whitey Morris and Poke Hasslin. They'll kind of entertain you till I come back with the sawbones that's gonna amputate your ears!"

Whitey Morris was a big tow-headed thug with a battered and ugly countenance. He said, "Killer Klaw, huh? It'll be a pleasure!"

Powers nodded, grinning. "Lay him on the cot and tie him up good. Gag him, and cover his face with a sheet. The saw-bones don't wanna see the face of the guy whose ears he amputates. That way, he'll never be able to talk about it. See?"

Whitey and Poke came over and seized Steve Klaw by the arms, keeping their guns out in their free hands. Powers closed the door connecting the living-room with the kitchen. Then he crossed and went out through the rear service entrance.

"I'll bring the doc up the back way," he said. He turned and went out.

When he was gone, Whitey Morris smirked and said, "Lay down on the cot, sucker. This is gonna be real fun. The doc says you won't need no anesthetic—so long as you're gagged good, and can't yell!"

"Yeah!" said Poke Hasslin. "And after we're through with you, comes more fun. We finish up Mannie an' his wife—and the two kids. The boss says it's got to be a lesson to squealers. There won't be no guys squawking on the boss—not after they hear what happened to Mannie and his family!"

Stephen Klaw was alongside the cot when Poke said that. His face congealed into a sudden terrible mask.

"You're going to knock off those two kids anyway?" he asked.

158

"Sure. Why not? You was a sucker to let Barney take you over. You should've known he wouldn't leave no witnesses alive."

"I see," said Steve. "Thanks for telling me. It makes a difference."

"Difference? Whadda you mean?"

"I mean *this!*" said Steve.

Both his arms twisted upward and outward in a windmill-like motion which tore their grip from his sleeves. His right fist, smashing backward, drove full into the face of Poke Hasslin. Poke staggered backward, thrown off balance by the surprise attack.

Whitey Morris twisted around to turn his gun on Steve, but Steve kicked him hard in the shins. Whitey screeched with the sharp pain. Almost before the screech was out of his mouth, Klaw dove in at him with a hard right to the pit of the stomach. Steve's fist almost buried itself in his abdomen. Whitey's breath left his body all in one *whoosh*. He doubled over, dropping the gun.

Stephen Klaw dropped to the floor on top of that gun, and rolled over, with the weapon in his fist. He came up facing Poke Hasslin, who had recovered his balance and was swinging his own gun to bear on Steve.

Steve grinned thinly, and kept the muzzle pointing at Hasslin, with his finger on the trigger. Hasslin yelled, "Wait! Don't shoot!" and let go of his gun as if it were white-hot steel. He spread his hands out. "I quit!"

STEPHEN KLAW came slowly to his feet. He threw a contemptuous glance at Hasslin. Then he looked down at

Whitey Morris, who was twisting on the floor in agonized contortions.

"Get on the cot, Whitey," he said in a voice entirely bereft of emotion.

Whitey raised pain-wracked eyes. "What—what you want me to do that for?"

"Get on the cot!" Steve repeated.

Whitey Morris gasped as Steve stepped in and raised the revolver to slash down at his face. "Wait! I'll get—on!"

He climbed onto the cot, and lay down on his back. Steve motioned to Poke Hasslin with the gun. "Tie him up!"

Almost eagerly, Hasslin hastened to obey. He got Whitey securely tied.

"Now gag him!"

A sudden terrible light of understanding came into Whitey's eyes. "Gawd, no! My ears—"

Poke Hasslin was so anxious to please Stephen Klaw that he didn't even give Whitey a chance to finish. He stuck the gag in his mouth, almost choking him, and tied it hard. Then, at Steve's direction, he covered Whitey's face with the sheet, leaving only the ears exposed.

Steve nodded. "That'll do fine!" He picked up the gun Poke Hasslin had dropped. "Now—go in the living-room. I'll be right behind you. Sudsy and Miklis are in there, holding guns on the two Roche kids. If you give them any kind of sign that causes them to shoot those kids, that'll be my cue to blast you in the back!"

"I won't, Klaw," Poke blubbered. "I swear I won't!"

He pushed the door open, and stepped slowly through into the living-room. Stephen Klaw's slim figure was entirely hidden behind the bulk of his body. Sudsy Fiorio and Jake Miklis hardly gave Hasslin more than a glance. They were holding the boy and the girl, and keeping Mannie and Flo motionless against the wall.

"Did they cut his ears off yet, Poke?" Fiorio asked.

"Not yet, my friend!" Stephen Klaw said softly. He stepped out from behind Hasslin. He was in back of the sofa now, to the right of Fiorio and Miklis. Sudsy Fiorio was nearest to him, and Jake Miklis was just beyond Sudsy.

Steve stepped out lithely. His gun rose and fell with a swift, ruthless chopping stroke. The barrel struck at a slant against the muscle in the upper part of Fiorio's arms, between the elbow and the shoulder. It paralyzed his entire arm, preventing him from shooting the revolver which he was holding at the base of the boy's head. Then with a swift flowing motion that seemed to blend both blows into one, Steve smashed downward with the gun in his other hand, bringing the barrel crashing against Sudsy's temple. Fiorio just gasped, and fell forward over the couch, letting the gun slide from paralyzed fingers.

Jake Miklis swung around, snarling with terror. He was holding onto the little girl's hair with his left hand, and he twisted the gun in his right toward Steve. But he was too late. His instinct had been wrong. He should have kept his gun trained on the child. That would have been a far more potent barrier between himself and Stephen Klaw than the muzzle of a revolver.

Klaw's eyes were hard and sharp. He fired both guns at the

same time, and both slugs buried themselves in the chest of Jake Miklis.

Miklis crashed backward, and stretched at full length on the floor, with blood spurting out of him like twin geysers.

Steve Klaw turned to cover Poke Hasslin, but that was unnecessary. Hasslin was thoroughly cowed. He had not made a move to escape or to attack. He just stood, motionless and licked.

Florence Roche choked back a little sob and ran over and put her arms around the two children, hugging them to her breast. Mannie's face was working spasmodically with unrepressed emotion. He came and put his hand on his wife's head, and stroked her hair. He looked over at Stephen Klaw, tears in his eyes.

"I—I can't believe it, Mister Klaw," he stammered. "I c-can't believe we're all safe—"

"We're not safe by a long shot!" Steve told him gruffly. "Didn't you hear what Powers said on the phone—when he talked to that boss of his? Their mob has taken over the building. We'd have to fight our way out—and what chance would your wife and kids have?"

He motioned to Hasslin to open the kitchen door. "Push it open and step out of the way. If Barney Powers has come up yet with that doctor, there'll be a little shooting."

Poke Hasslin turned the knob of the kitchen door, and pushed. His face became puzzled.

"It won't open! The catch must have clicked, and locked it from the other side!"

Steve sprang across and tried it. The door would not open. A single glance told him that the lock was a tumbler pattern which could not be picked.

Mannie Roche was at his side, whispering, "Nobody could open that without a key. I had it put on myself, because I had to talk to some of the mob in the kitchen, and I wanted privacy."

"Then you have the key!"

"No, Mister Klaw. Powers took my keys when we came in."

"I see," said Steve. "Well—"

He broke off short, at the sound of loud voices in the kitchen, through the closed door:

"Okay, Doc? Both ears, huh?" It was voice of Barney Powers, gloating.

The doctor answered, "A perfect amputation, Barney. Here, I've cauterized the ears, and I'll put them in the shoebox for you. That'll be a fee of five hundred dollars."

"All right, Doc—here you are. I wonder what happened to Poke and Whitey. They must be next door with the rest of the gang.... *Hey!* This ain't Klaw! This is Whitey! My Gawd, Doc, you cut off Whitey Morris's ears!"

"Well, it's not my fault, Barney. You told me not to take the sheet off the man's face—"

"Shut up, damn you. Klaw must be next door. Now I know what happened. I should have got an army to hold that Killer Klaw. Well, he won't get away. The building is covered. I got machine-guns on every floor. What's done is done. I'll send Whitey's ears in the shoebox. Those two G-men won't know the difference. They'll think it's Klaw's ears, and they'll come anyway!"

163

STEPHEN KLAW'S hand tightened on the gun. He motioned everybody in the room to stand back, and aimed the revolver at the lock. "Got to break through," he muttered to Mannie. "Or else Powers will have Kerrigan and Murdoch walking into this trap!"

But Mannie Roche put a hasty hand on his arm. "It's no use, Mister Klaw. I had that door put on special—same with the front door. They're lined with that new kind of steel—bullet-proof and ax-proof. The lock, too. It'll only jam, but it'll never open. Barney Powers knows that. He gave orders for all the guys in the mob to equip their houses like this—in case of trouble."

Steve Klaw shrugged, and lowered the gun. He looked over at Poke Hasslin, who was sitting disconsolately in a corner. Florence Roche was on the sofa, holding her two children close. She smiled at Steve—wanly but bravely.

Steve went over to the telephone, and lifted it off the cradle. He held it to his ear for a while. Then, very slowly, he put it down. He didn't need to tell them. They knew from his expression that the phone was dead.

Florence Roche's eyes were bright with faith. "You'll find a way out, Mister Klaw—I'm sure of it. You are a good man, and God is with you!" she told him.

Steve felt a little tug at his heart. He wanted to tell her that there wasn't much chance. Mannie Roche knew that. He knew how Barney Powers worked. And Barney Powers had the backing of Milo Flinders. Powers might slip—but Flinders wouldn't.

Steve's lips were tight. He came around in front of the couch and smiled down at the boy and girl.

Ronnie was blond, like his father, with sensitive, intelligent features. Little May was pretty, with dark ringlets framing a thin, delicate oval of face. She had her mother's features, and Steve could see that Florence Roche must have been very beautiful before worry and care robbed her of her looks.

Ronnie sat up straight, and met Steve's gaze with wide-open, worshiping eyes. May put out a hand and touched his sleeve.

"I like you," she said. "You stopped that bad man who was holding me by the hair."

Steve stroked her head. Then he gave Ronnie a little slap on the back. "Chin up, kids," he said. "Nobody's going to bother you any more if I can help it."

He left them, and went over to the window. Mannie Roche joined him.

"This window opens on an inside airshaft," he said. "The one on the other side faces the river. The bedroom window faces the same way."

"What about fire escapes?" Steve asked.

Mannie shook his head. "This is a fireproof house. There's a fire-exit in the rear—through the kitchen."

Steve pulled aside the shade a quarter of an inch, and applied his eye to it. "It's dark in the airshaft. If Powers is as thorough as I figure him, he'll have someone posted in that opposite window—"

His words were drowned by a crashing fusillade of shots from the darkened window on the other side of the airshaft. Bullets crashed the glass, pierced the shade, and spattered against the far wall.

Steve Klaw ducked back and threw Mannie Roche out of the way. Luckily, the couch on which Flo was sitting with the two children was over near the side wall. But Poke Hasslin's chair was directly opposite the window. He fell over with a choked cry, blood pouring from his face and neck.

The firing kept up for another minute, then stopped.

Steve was hugging the wall alongside the window. As soon as the shooting ceased, he thrust one of his revolvers through the broken glass, and fired five times fast into the darkened window opposite.

Someone screamed, and a gun clattered against the side of the building, then landed with a thud of shattering metal on the concrete floor of the airshaft, six stories below.

"That takes care of one of them!" Steve said grimly. He got Mannie to help, and they moved a tall sideboard up against the window. Then he went over and examined Poke Hasslin. The man was dead.

Sudsy Fiorio was just beginning to stir, so Steve and Mannie tied him up with strips of a sheet. Then they herded Flo and the children into the bedroom.

Back in the living-room, Mannie got out a bottle of whiskey, and poured two drinks with a shaking hand.

"What're we gonna do, Mister Klaw? Wait here till they come for us?"

Steve shrugged. "If it weren't for Flo and the kids, we'd open the front door and shoot our way down to the street. We might not get there, but we'd take a few of that mob along. As it is, we just have to sit tight. Johnny Kerrigan and Dan Murdoch will surely come walking into this trap. I wish I could figure some way of warning them. If there was only a window opening on the front."

"What about all that shooting?" Mannie asked hopefully. "There's a cop on this beat."

"For the cop's sake," Steve said, "I hope he didn't hear the shots. If he should try to investigate, he'll probably get a slug in the back!"

His glance fastened thoughtfully on the airshaft window, barricaded with the bureau.

"If we put out the light in this room, Mannie—and if you could start shooting across at that window opposite, so as to keep those muggs occupied—maybe I could shinny down to the ground on a rope."

"Where are we gonna get the rope?"

"Have you got a lot of bedsheets? We could tear them in strips—"

"They'd never hold you for six flights, Mister Klaw. And anyway, even if I could keep the guys opposite busy, there'll be more of 'em down below. They'd get you."

Stephen Klaw's eyes were glinting. "It's worth a try, Mannie. Otherwise, Kerrigan and Murdoch will get the works—and then they'll come for us."

"But suppose the rope breaks—or suppose they're waiting for you at the bottom and shoot you before you get to the ground?"

Steve shrugged. "It's better than waiting here—and doing nothing." He gave Mannie Roche a little push. "Go in the bedroom and get your wife to rustle up all the sheets she can find!"

CHAPTER 5
THE JAWS OF THE TRAP

A THOUSAND feet away from the Shore-crest Apartments, was the construction shack which Mannie Roche had pointed out to Stephen Klaw. That shack was now the scene of unusual activity, for Milo Flinders had made it his temporary headquarters.

The single window was carefully boarded up so that no light could shine through from the bulb hanging above the crude table in the center of the room. Before that table sat Milo Flinders. His long, thin fingers were drumming impatiently on the top. His eyes were gentle, deceiving. But his lips were set in a hard, cruel line as he looked across at Barney Powers, who stood facing him, shuffling nervously.

"I couldn't help it, boss," Powers was saying. "The doc cut Whitey's ears off before I knew who was under that sheet. But what the hell—Kerrigan and Murdoch won't know the difference. They'll come all right."

"We shall soon see," Milo Flinders murmured. He glanced at his wrist watch. "It's almost eleven-thirty—ample time for them to have received the package, and to get here. Have you made all arrangements?"

"Yes, Boss. I got thirty men in that building, with machine-guns and sawed-off shotguns. Once Kerrigan and Murdoch get in there, they'll never get out alive."

"What about the other tenants?"

Powers grinned. "My boys are taking care of them. They told the tenants, if they poke their noses out the door, it's curtains. I got men in one apartment on each floor, to cut off Kerrigan and Murdoch so they can't get out again. And I got men in the apartment opposite Mannie's, on the sixth floor. It faces Mannie's window across the airshaft. Then there's two machine-gunners on the sixth floor, with guns trained on Mannie's door. If Klaw tries to come out that way, he'll just be walking into a lead shower."

Flinders nodded. "You cut off the telephone service?"

"Right, Boss. I shorted the cable. No calls can go out of there. And I got a man with a field-glass just outside the shack, watching the street. As soon as he sees Kerrigan and Murdoch coming—"

He was interrupted by the opening of the shack door. A gorilla with a field-glass poked his face in. "Barney! Here they come!"

Milo Flinders' hands clenched on the table-top. "Ah! I knew they'd rise to the bait! Well, there's nothing to do but watch the famous Suicide Squad march its last mile!"

He put out the light, and went to the door with Barney. Just outside the shack, a dozen men were huddled together. They were thugs from another outfit, which Flinders had hastily gathered to reinforce Barney's decimated gang. They all carried rifles, and were eagerly watching a cab that had pulled up at the corner, a hundred feet from the Shore-crest Apartments. Two men got slowly out of the cab.

Flinders seized the field-glasses from the lookout, and applied them to his own eyes.

"That's Kerrigan and Murdoch, all right!" he said with satisfaction. He watched the two G-men pay off their cab and start to walk slowly toward the Shore-crest.

"Look, Boss," said Barney Powers, "I'm a crack shot with a rifle. Lemme pick them off from here."

"No!" said Flinders. "You might get one, but the other would escape. And it's necessary to kill them all. One of those three devils remaining alive to avenge his two companions would be more dangerous to us than a whole pack of wildcats. We stay here and wait—and if, by some wild chance, they manage to escape the trap in the house, we'll get them on the way out. Barney, I'm making absolutely certain that this is the end of the Suicide Squad!"

DOWN IN the street, Johnny Kerrigan and Dan Murdoch were moving carefully and warily. Murdoch was white with rage, Kerrigan boiling over with fury. They had just heard a news item on the taxicab radio, which accounted for their murderous mood. The eleven o'clock train to Washington had stopped at Newark. Five men armed with sub-machine guns had invaded Car 14. They had ripped open the door of Compartment A. Without a word of warning, they had turned loose their sub-machine guns upon the two occupants of the compartment, who had been asleep, riddling them with more than fifty shots. Then the five desperados had left. On the way out they had encountered

Sam Lake, a Negro porter, who was carrying a brief-case which probably belonged to some passenger. For no known reason, the desperados had opened up on poor Sam Lake, cutting him down with a stream of bullets. Then they had snatched the brief-case and made good their escape from the train.

That was the gist of the news-flash on the radio. And the two G-men had been barely able to contain themselves as they listened.

"Now the evidence is gone," Dan Murdoch said bitterly. "The only thing that could have convicted Milo Flinders. We have to start all over again from scratch. And poor Sam Lake is dead. I feel like a murderer."

"By God," said Johnny Kerrigan as they walked slowly toward the apartment house, "we'll make it up to Sam somehow. We'll find out if he had a family. Maybe we can get them a pension. After all, Sam died in the service of the F.B.I."

"Better pay attention to what we're doing right now," Dan Murdoch said dryly. "Or we'll never get a chance to do anything for Sam's family. There's the house Mannie Roche lives in. If I figure right, the Shrimp is in there—without his ears."

Johnny nodded. "And there's a hellish little trap of some kind waiting for us." His eyes glittered. "Come on, Dan. Let's get it over with!"

They stood before the entrance of the Shore-crest Apartments.

"Something tells me," said Johnny, "that we should have asked for a raiding party. This is more than a two-man job. We're up against a bigger brain than Barney Powers. Milo Flinders must have worked this out."

Murdoch shook his head. "Squad cars would be spotted five miles away. They'd clear out and leave nothing for us to find. Flinders couldn't have picked a better location if he'd planned this months ahead!"

Johnny Kerrigan took one of his guns out, "Okay. Let's go in."

Dan Murdoch said quietly, "Wait."

He was looking up at the face of the tall building. "Take a squint, Johnny. Do you notice anything strange about this place?"

Kerrigan followed his glance, frowning. "No."

"Isn't it funny that there isn't a light showing in any of those windows? It's not even midnight. Surely all the tenants don't go to sleep this early."

"Meaning what?"

Murdoch shrugged. "It might mean that Flinders has taken over the building. He's done it before. We might be walking into to a nest of sub-machine guns in the lobby."

"To hell with that. Let's go in and find out what they've done to the Shrimp."

"Not both of us, Johnny. I'll go in the front way. You go around the back. If they start shooting when I come in, you take them in the rear—"

"Nix. *I* go in the front way!"

Murdoch sighed. "Okay. We toss."

He spun a coin. Kerrigan called, Heads."

It came out a tail. Murdoch grinned. "The back way for you, Kerrigan, my bucko!"

Johnny scowled. "All right. We meet in the lobby, and go up together. Give me a chance to find the back entrance before you go in. What do you say?"

"Right."

Kerrigan started walking toward the far side of the building. "So long, Dan. See you in hell."

"See you in hell, Johnny," echoed Murdoch. He lit a cigarette and puffed it, giving his partner time to get around to the rear. He stood tensely, with the guns in his shoulder holsters eased forward so that the tops of their butts almost protruded from under his coat. He let his eyes flicker up and down the dark and deserted street.

Far below, over the river, he caught the lights of a ferry, crawling across the Jersey shore like an immense, squat tortoise. An excursion boat, brilliantly illuminated, was working down the river. Life, and gayety, and music. While up here on the bleak cliffs above the city, there was stalking peril and lurking death.

Murdoch smiled grimly, and threw away the cigarette. He drew both guns and walked into the lobby of the Shore-crest Apartments.

THE LOBBY was deserted. A chandelier in the center threw light in every corner. No one was lurking here. The door of the self-service elevator stood open and inviting. At the right of the elevator shaft there was another door, which would probably lead to the rear, or to the basement. On either side of the lobby were the doors of the ground-floor flats—four in all.

Murdoch stood very still, waiting. Presently he saw the rear door begin to inch open. First the muzzle of a revolver appeared in the opening—then the face of Johnny Kerrigan.

The big blond G-man came into the lobby, grinning.

"Nothing so far, Dan. Not a soul out in back. There's light in one apartment in the rear—on the sixth floor. That'll be Mannie Roche's."

Murdoch nodded. His eyes kept swiveling from one closed apartment door to another, waiting for the expected attack. He motioned toward the self-service elevator. Johnny Kerrigan stepped into it. Murdoch turned around, and backed in after him. He reached over and pushed the button for '6.' The door slid shut, and the cage started to rise.

"Nuts!" said Johnny Kerrigan. "This is too easy. Nobody's even trying to stop us."

"That's what I'm afraid of," Murdoch murmured. "Keep on your toes when we get out at the sixth—"

Suddenly the cage shuddered, and came to a jarring stop. They were between the fourth and fifth floors.

Murdoch's eyes narrowed. He pressed the button again. Nothing happened.

"Somebody's shut off the power," said Kerrigan. "We're stuck. No way to get out."

"Well," Murdoch grinned wryly, "we walked into it all right. Like a couple of prize saps."

"How will they get to us, though?" asked Johnny. "They'll have to come after us. We'll see them as soon as they see us. And we can still pull a mean trigger."

Almost before he finished speaking, there was a loud, nearly deafening, hissing sound from somewhere below.

"Escaping steam!" Murdoch exclaimed. "There's your answer, Johnny. They're deflecting the steam from the boiler-room into this shaft!"

"I get it, Dan. Boiled alive, huh?"

White steam began to percolate through the grating in the sides of the cage. It began to get unbearably hot. Kerrigan looked down at his gun and saw moisture forming on the metal.

Dan Murdoch started to laugh.

Kerrigan glared at him. "What's so funny?"

"I was just thinking," said Dan, "what a nice dish we'll make for Milo Flinders—steamed G-men on toast!" He laughed.

Johnny grinned. "Well, I guess it's all over, Dan. We had a good time while it lasted. Somebody was bound to get us sooner or later. Only I'd rather take lead in the guts than be cooked alive."

"Well," said Murdoch, weighing his guns, "we could do it."

It was getting so hot that their collars were wilting. Their faces were covered with sweat. They had to look at each other through a hazy fog of hot stifling steam which enveloped them.

Johnny Kerrigan looked down at his gun. "It would be an easy way out, Dan. I only wish I knew what happened to the Shrimp."

"We'll probably meet him in hell. If we want to do this thing, Johnny, we got to do it fast. The cartridges will start exploding in the guns by themselves in a couple of minutes. It'll be too late then.

Kerrigan said slowly, "One of us would have to do it to the other—and then to himself."

Murdoch nodded. "We could toss."

"Okay, Dan. You toss. I'll cry. And I hope to heaven you win!"

Slowly, Dan Murdoch took out the coin which he had tossed before. He flipped it up in the air....

CHAPTER 6
"HI, MOPES!"

STEPHEN KLAW shimmied down the rope carefully, testing each knot before he passed it. It had taken six bedsheets, twisted into rope and then knotted end-to-end to reach the ground. Looking upward, Klaw could see Mannie Roche's white face peering down. Just behind Mannie, he glimpsed Flo, who was also watching. Instead of going down the airshaft, Steve had decided to drop the improvised rope from the rear bedroom window. He couldn't be sure that it would reach the ground, but he was taking that chance. At the worst, he'd have to kick in a first-floor window, and climb in.

But the rope just made it. He had only a three or four foot drop to the ground. He tugged three times hard on the rope, and Mannie Roche hauled it up again.

Stephen Klaw was alone in the rear courtyard of the house. He stood there for a minute, listening for signs of watchers, but there were none.

What he did hear was a loud hissing noise, which continued and grew in volume. At first he couldn't identify it, then decided that it was steam escaping from the boiler. Probably something wrong with the heating system. No time to investigate that now....

He made his way along a narrow alley, and found the rear door to the lobby. He pushed it open a crack, and his nostrils were at once assailed by the dense, hot stench of live steam. There was a good deal of it in the lobby, and it seemed to be seeping out from the elevator shaft.

For a moment. Steve waited without opening the door further. He was puzzled by the steam. He started to push the door open, then caught himself in time.

Men were coming into the lobby—a half-dozen of them, carrying sub-machineguns and sawed-off shotguns. At their head was Barney Powers.

Powers strode in, and stood, grinning like a death's head. "Well," he said to the men with him, "I guess that does the trick. Kerrigan and Murdoch are in the elevator. In ten minutes they'll be steamed beef. My engineer down in the cellar knows his business all right."

Stephen Klaw, crouching behind the partly open door, stiffened.

"We'll wait till we're sure they're dead," said Powers. "Then we'll go up and blast the door off Mannie's apartment."

Steve Klaw watched, tensely. If Kerrigan and Murdoch were trapped in that elevator, he'd have to shut off the steam. His eye, at the crack in the door, focused on another door in the opposite corner of the lobby. The lettering upon it said, Boiler Room.

To get there, Steve would have to cross the lobby—a lobby

filled with a half-dozen heavily armed gangsters. And he'd have to do it fast. He knew Kerrigan and Murdoch. They wouldn't wait to be steamed alive. They'd finish it quickly, with bullets in their brains.

Internally, Stephen Klaw was seething with desperation. Externally, he was cool and collected. He took from his pockets his available artillery, which consisted of two revolvers—one taken from Fiorio, the other from Miklis. Both guns were fully loaded.

Stephen Klaw gripped the two guns, then kicked the door wide open!

TO THOSE gangsters assembled in the lobby, Klaw must have seemed like some avenging demon from the nether regions. His face was set in an unyielding mask. His eyes, slate-gray and hard, were the sinister eyes of Killer Klaw, of whom men talked in hushed voices. He stood there in the doorway, unmoving and immovable, with legs far apart and the two guns spitting hot lead. He offered no quarter, and asked for none. He fired and fired, and kept on firing until his guns were empty.

But with all the desperate rage that encompassed his soul, Stephen Klaw was yet the cold and calculating fighting man. He made each shot count. Men fell before those two terrible blasting guns, before they could bring their own weapons into play. Afterwards it was revealed that not a single shot had been fired by the mobsters.

So great was their terror at the sudden apparition of the man whom they had thought to be safely trapped in the apartment upstairs, that their muscles refused to obey the orders of their brains. Those who could, dropped their weapons and fled for their lives.

When Stephen Klaw stopped shooting, four of them lay dead, and the body of a fifth choked the doorway to the street. The sixth was painfully dragging his wounded body down the street, and the seventh—Barney Powers himself—was standing in a corner of the lobby with his hands thrust high in the air in token of surrender.

Stephen Klaw's lips twisted in a dreadful grin. He sprang across the lobby to where Powers stood. He threw away his empty guns.

The eyes of Barney Powers opened wide when he saw that. A crafty gleam came into them. His hands dropped swiftly, the right streaking to a shoulder holster which he had feared to use before.

But Stephen Klaw stepped in lightly and expertly. A left jab straightened Powers' head. A right came crashing up against Powers' jaw.

Barney Powers' body arced over backward from the force of that blow. Teeth crunched hard. Blood dripped from his mouth. His shoulders sagged, and he seemed to congeal into himself. Stephen Klaw had put all his hatred and rage behind the punch. And Barney Powers lay still on the floor at his feet.

Steve wasted no more precious seconds. He stooped swiftly and ran fingers through Powers' pockets. He grunted with satisfaction when he found his own automatics, which Powers had taken from him. Then he brought out a pair of handcuffs, dragged the unconscious man over to the elevator shaft, and handcuffed him to the grating. The steam was coming through stronger now, and Barney would get a little of his own medicine for a while.

Then Klaw dashed across the lobby and pulled open the door of the boiler-room. There was a steep set of iron stairs, and he literally flew down them. At the bottom he saw a man in shirtsleeves standing near the boiler—a gun in one hand, the other on the steam-pressure gauge.

The man turned at the sound of Steve's racing feet. One glance was enough for him. He lifted up his gun and pressed the trigger. Steve fired four times fast with his right-hand automatic, and the man went down with every one of the four slugs less than an inch apart in his heart.

Klaw stepped over the prostrate body and snatched at the steam gauge, pulling the lever all the way down to zero. The hissing of the steam stopped.

There was an electric switch-box on one wall, containing eight or nine switches. Steve closed all the open circuits, returning the power to the lines. He heard the rumbling of the elevator.

By the time he got out of the boiler-room and back into the lobby, the cage was down at the ground floor. The door slid open, and Kerrigan and Murdoch felt their way out amid clouds of steam.

Their faces and necks were red like boiled lobsters.

"It's the Shrimp!" yelled Johnny Kerrigan. He came over and pawed at Klaw, feeling his ears. "And he's all in one piece!"

Dan Murdoch smiled. "Hi, Shrimp."

"Hi, Mopes," said Stephen Klaw.

HE GRINNED as he inserted new clips in his automatics. "There's a lot of rats in this building," he told them. "Let's go and clean them out." But it wasn't necessary. A police riot car came screaming up to the entrance, followed by a hook-and-ladder company, and a couple of hose trucks.

"What brought you guys?" Steve Klaw demanded of the firemen.

"What brought us!" exclaimed the fire captain. He pointed to the steam hissing out of the elevator shaft. "There's a column of smoke pouring out of this building that can be seen down at the Battery!"

And then a strange thing happened. Tenants of the building came trooping down the stairs, carrying whatever belongings they could snatch up. The clang of the engines had made them believe that the house was afire.

Kerrigan and Murdoch and Klaw herded the tenants out, questioning each one, and demanding identification. In that way they rounded up most of the gunmen, who had no fight left in them at all. In fact, they had abandoned their machineguns upstairs.

Steve Klaw himself brought the Roche family down. They were dazed, hardly able to believe that they had come out of the terrible experience alive.

The police had brought up the wagons and were loading the prisoners into them.

"Take 'em all," said Stephen Klaw, "except this one—" pointing to Barney Powers. "He comes to Washington with me.

We'll give him a nice cell in the Federal Detention House there. Maybe he'll decide to talk a little—about Milo Flinders!"

"To hell with you," said Barney Powers, as Steve took the handcuffs off him and pulled him away from the elevator shaft. "I want a lawyer!"

"You'll get one," Steve said softly.

"That's the trouble," Kerrigan growled. "A rat like him gets every break. What break did they give poor Sam Lake?"

"What do you mean?" Steve asked.

Kerrigan told him about receiving the ears, and about Sam's murder on the train.

Steve's face was white. "Boys," he said, "we'll attend Sam's funeral in Washington tomorrow. Then we're going to get Milo Flinders."

CHAPTER 7
VENGEANCE FOR
THE F.B.I. DEAD!

THE FUNERAL cortège came to a halt outside the cemetery. With bared heads, a hundred G-men followed the coffin of Sam Lake, formerly a porter for the Pullman Company, but a hero in death. He was being buried with the full honors of one who has died in the service of the United States of America. A file of riflemen from the third cavalry post stood by to fire a last salute. Dozens of officials and business men from Washington had come to this little cemetery across the Potomac to pay tribute to a lowly porter.

But of all those present, none attracted so much curious and avid attention as the three men who stood in a compact little group alongside the grave.

Probably everyone there was talking about those three men.

"They're the Suicide Squad—Kerrigan, Murdoch and Klaw. Queer—those three devils are always casting dice with Death, yet Death loses...."

Among those who were watching from a little distance was another man who did not attract so much attention from the crowd. His silvery hair, general air of dignity and probity, bespoke a respectable, prosperous business man.

But the eyes of Kerrigan, Murdoch and Klaw kept constantly reverting to him.

Milo Flinders was smug and dignified. The F.B.I. had nothing against him. There was no longer any evidence anywhere that might convict him. And although he seemed to share the general sorrow at the death of Sam Lake, there was yet a gleam in his eye which belied that attitude.

Not far from where Kerrigan, Murdoch and Klaw stood, there was another group—one which kept looking almost worshipfully at Stephen Klaw. Mannie and Florence Roche, with Ronnie and May. They had been brought to Washington after being evacuated from the Shore-crest Apartments, and Mannie had already been promised a job as an automobile mechanic with one of the Capitol taxicab concerns—a job with which he was familiar, for he had been a mechanic before he got into the rackets.

The gathered citizens listened with shining eyes to the peroration which the Director of the F.B.I. delivered over the grave of Sam Lake, and then they saw him walk sternly over to the Suicide Squad. They saw that his face was lined with care. But they did not hear the words that he spoke.

"I hope you boys noticed who's here," he said, jerking his head in the direction of Milo Flinders.

"Damn him!" muttered Johnny Kerrigan. "How can he have the gall to come to the funeral of a man whose death he ordered? Maybe he didn't give the orders in so many words. But it was his gunmen that killed Sam Lake!"

"And now," said the Director, "Milo Flinders goes scot free, I suppose?" He turned a baleful eye on Kerrigan and Murdoch. "If you two men hadn't turned back to help Klaw, Sam Lake would be alive today."

Dan Murdoch lowered his eyes. "You're right, sir. And I think someone should pay off for Sam. If you'll give me permission to resign, sir, I'd like to have the status of a private citizen—"

"So you can walk up to Milo Flinders and shoot him?" the Director asked bitterly.

Dan Murdoch shuffled uncomfortably. "Well, not exactly, sir. I've been thinking of resigning for quite a while. There are certain private matters—"

"Never mind stalling, Murdoch," said his superior. "I know what's in your mind. You've been thinking of resigning ever since Sam was killed. You want to be free to murder Flinders. Well, forget it. I've got only one order for you three—*get Milo Flinders*. Get evidence against him!"

"How would it be sir," Stephen Klaw asked, "if Milo Flinders were to attempt to kill one of us three, and the other two were forced to—er—sort of eliminate him in self-defense?"

The Director scowled at Klaw. "You've a bad enough reputation as a killer right now."

"I wouldn't touch him, sir," said Steve. "I'd be the fall guy. Dan and Johnny could take care of him."

The Director sighed. "You three are hopeless. I think I'll assign other men to this case. It'll keep you out of trouble; I'm sending you to the Chicago office in the morning. Report at ten o'clock tomorrow for orders. In the meantime, consider yourselves relieved of duty!"

"But, sir…." Stephen Klaw started to protest, but found himself talking to the Director's back.

The crowd was already leaving the cemetery. Milo Flinders was gone.

Klaw turned and looked at his two partners. He shrugged. "Well," he said, "that's that. It's the first case we've flopped on— *if* we quit."

"What do you mean—*if?*" Johnny Kerrigan demanded. "You heard the chief's orders. We're relieved of duty till the morning."

"Exactly!" Steve murmured. "We're on our own till ten o'clock tomorrow."

"I get it," said Dan Murdoch. His dark eyes glittered.

"So do I," growled Johnny Kerrigan. He started to grin broadly. "So what are we waiting for?"

With one accord the three turned and hurried from the cemetery. As they stepped away from the grave of Sam Lake, they stopped for a minute, came gravely to attention, and saluted.

Then they got into their car and Johnny Kerrigan took the wheel. He headed back to Washington.

Their first stop was at the office of a certain criminal attorney by the name of Jerome Usher, who owed the three of them a great many favors….

BARNEY POWERS was not exactly the happiest man in the world. Quickly after his capture in the Shore-crest Apartments, he had been hustled to Washington under close guard, and placed incommunicado in a cell in the Federal Detention House.

Having been here for twenty-four hours, he was beginning to wonder when he'd get out. It was true that there were plenty of charges to hang on him. The fight in his barroom, his threats against the two children of Mannie Roche, and his subsequent attempt to steam Kerrigan and Murdoch alive. But he wasn't much worried by any of them. There were no witnesses against him except the three F.B.I. men, and the family of Mannie Roche. Seven people in all. He was confident that Milo Flinders would manage to eliminate all seven of them in some way before the trial.

Flinders had to do it, or else Powers could talk plenty. Of course, Flinders hadn't been able to bail him out yet, because the G-men hadn't announced where they were keeping him. But they couldn't keep him incommunicado forever. As soon as Flinders' underground wires brought in the news of where Barney Powers was being held, the boss would bail him out. No doubt the boss was attending the funeral of that dub, Sam Lake, today, in the hope of picking up some dope. The boss was clever, all right. You couldn't beat his system. Maybe that stunt had flopped up at the Shore-crest Apartments—but Flinders would keep trying, and the Suicide Squad would get theirs in the end!

In the meantime, all he had to do was sit tight and keep mum. It was a good thing these G-men weren't allowed to use the 'third degree.' They couldn't make him talk….

Barney's thoughts were interrupted by the opening of his cell door.

"Come on!" said the jailer.

Barney Powers followed the jailer down the cell tier and into the office. His eyes lighted as he saw the familiar figure of Jerome Usher, the celebrated criminal lawyer, talking to the warden.

"Mr. Usher here," said the warden, frowning, "has just furnished bail for you, Powers. You are free to go. Your bond requires that you appear for a hearing before a United States Commissioner within forty-eight hours. In the meantime, please understand that you are not to leave the District of Columbia."

"Sure, sure!" grinned Barney Powers, as he followed Jerome Usher out of the office.

As they descended the steps of the jail building, Barney even swaggered a little. "I knew I'd get out, Mr. Usher," he boasted. "Did the boss send you?"

Jerome Usher raised his eyebrows. "You ask too many questions," he said coldly. "Just get into this car at the curb, and you will be taken to your destination."

Powers scowled. "You don't have to talk so high-and-mighty, guy. I ain't small potatoes."

"Undoubtedly not," said Jerome Usher, guiding him up to the long black car at the curb. "Just get in."

The door was opened by someone on the inside, and Powers put a foot on the running-board. Then he saw who was in the car. The marrow congealed in his bones…. He started to back out.

"Nix—"

But the long arm of Johnny Kerrigan reached out and gripped him by the lapels, yanked him in. He was rudely plopped down in the back seat between Kerrigan and Murdoch.

"Lemme go!" he yelled. "I don't wanta be bailed out—"

Johnny Kerrigan sighed. "Shows you how ungrateful a guy can be!" He grabbed Powers by the back of the neck, and stuffed a handkerchief into his mouth.

Powers sputtered wildly.

"Naughty, naughty!" Johnny chided, and shoved the handkerchief in farther, effectively gagging him.

"Okay, Shrimp," he said to Steve Klaw at the wheel, "drive on!"

Klaw grinned at Jerome Usher, who did not get in the car.

"Thanks, Jerry," said Steve. "I'll do the same for you sometime!"

"Don't mention it, Steve. Always glad to bail your friends out!" Usher swung the door shut, and Steve drove away.

In the back, Barney Powers was in a bad way. He could neither move nor talk, for the grip of Johnny Kerrigan was powerful. Dan Murdoch, on his left, had quietly slipped a pair of bracelets on his wrists, so he was helpless.

STEVE KLAW drove across town for ten minutes. No one talked to Powers. They pulled up in a side street behind a tall apartment house, and without ceremony hustled Powers out of the car and into an alley, then down to the cellar. They brought him into a narrow storeroom, hardly large enough to hold them all. There was only a single chair in this cubicle, and Johnny Kerrigan plopped Powers into it.

Dan Murdoch deftly unfastened the handcuffs, then swung Barney's wrists behind his back and locked them again—with the chain running through the back slats. Kerrigan took the gag out of his mouth.

"Let me outta here!" Powers bellowed.

"Tut, tut," said Johnny. "Make yourself comfortable. You'll be here a while."

"A friend of mine is the super of this house," Murdoch explained courteously. "He lent us the use of the cellar for today. He's gone to visit an aunt in Baltimore. We won't be disturbed, I assured you."

Powers tried to rise, pulling the chair with him, but he found that the chair was fastened firmly to the floor. He couldn't move it.

"You guys think you're smart!" he snarled. "Well, you can't make me talk."

"All we want you to do," said Stephen Klaw, "is to sign a confession—detailing everything that you have done at the command of Milo Flinders."

"You're crazy!" Powers yelled. "I'll take a beating, but I won't sign my life away!"

Johnny Kerrigan looked shocked. "Beating! You don't think we'd lay a hand on you!"

Barney Powers' eyes grew narrow. "Then what'd you bail me out for?"

"Just to get your signed confession," was the answer. "You write it out and sign it. We give you our word that we'll return you to jail without harming you. You can claim later, that you signed it under duress. You know it would be no good in court."

Powers gave them a suspicious look. "And suppose I refuse? You won't beat me up?"

"Oh, no," Steve told him. "We'll just leave you here."

"I think the three of you are screwy. I won't sign nothing."

Stephen Klaw sighed. "All right, Powers. We'll be going. Come on, guys."

They started for the door. Murdoch and Kerrigan went out, grinning. Steve Klaw remained behind for a moment. He went to the corner opposite Powers' chair, and turned a valve on a steam pipe which ran through the room. Immediately, it began to hiss.

"Hey!" screamed Powers. "What's that?"

"Just live steam," Klaw explained to him, backing away from the stream of hot vapor which poured out of the pipe. "We're just leaving you here—with the steam. The way you left Kerrigan and Murdoch. Only in *your* case, no one is going to come and turn it off."

Stephen Klaw started for the door.

"Wait! God—wait!" shouted Powers. Klaw raised his eyebrows. "What's the matter, Barney? Can't you take it? A man should always be ready to take as good as he hands out. You ought to be ashamed of yourself."

The steam was rapidly filling the room. It was pouring out of the pipe in such a way that it passed within a foot of Barney Powers' helpless body. He would be well boiled in almost no time.

"T-turn it off!" he gasped. "I'll—sign—*anything!*"

CHAPTER 8
BULLET IN THE BACK

IT WAS almost three o'clock in the afternoon when Stephen Klaw rang the bell of Milo Flinders' terrace apartment on M Street Northwest.

The butler who opened the door was a husky, sour-faced man, whose features more closely resembled those of a footpad than of a gentleman's butler. There was a bulge under the left armpit of his uniform, which was hard to detect except by the expert eye.

Stephen Klaw said mildly, "They told me at the office that Mr. Flinders came directly home from the funeral. I should like to talk to him, please. My name is Klaw—Stephen Klaw, of the Federal Bureau of Investigation."

The butler nodded. "The office phoned. Mr. Flinders is expecting you."

Stephen Klaw followed him inside. There were two men in the foyer, sitting about idly, as if awaiting an interview with Flinders. Klaw knew them both, from photographs. They were ex-Chicago gangsters—men who had never been in the toils of the law, but who should have been. Klaw knew that Flinders employed bodyguards like these, changing them often, and getting them from the various gangs which he financed.

The two men looked at Klaw obliquely as he passed through, but gave no sign that they recognized him.

In the library, Milo Flinders sat behind a broad mahogany desk. He rose with a satiric smile of welcome, and waved to the butler to leave. When they were alone, he extended his hand across the desk.

"Glad to see you again, Klaw," he said. "The last time you were here, we had some pretty hot words. You made some accusations against me, and I defied you to prove them. I hope you've come to apologize."

Stephen Klaw's eyes were hard and cold.

"No, Flinders," he answered. "I've come to prove everything I said. I told you then, that you were the head of a vicious organization that financed rackets in every part of the country. I told you that you were responsible for many murders. Well, since then, you've added to the list. Your men killed Sam Lake. For that, I'm going to get you."

Milo Flinders raised his eyebrows. "Interesting—if true. What about the evidence you were going to get against me?"

"You got that evidence back—when Sam Lake was murdered. But I have new evidence against you. This morning, I caused Barney Powers to be bailed out."

He saw the visible start of surprise which Flinders was unable to repress. Then Flinders laughed. "Impossible!"

Steve pointed to the phone. "Use it. You can verify that very easily. Powers was being held in the Federal Detention House."

Milo Flinders ran a hand through his silvery hair. His keen, hawk-eyes studied Steve for a second. Then he picked up the phone and called a number. He spoke for only a minute, then hung up.

"That's right, Klaw. Powers was bailed out this morning. What happened to him?"

Steve grinned. "I took him on a little ride. He signed a full confession. Want to see it?"

From his pocket he took the confession which Powers had signed, and placed it carefully on the desk.

Flinders dropped his eyes, and read it slowly. When he finished, he looked up. He was smiling crookedly. "It appears to implicate me pretty thoroughly. Who else knows about this confession besides yourself?"

"No one has read it but me," Klaw said.

"Your two friends—Kerrigan and Murdoch?" Flinders' eyes raised.

"They're not in on this."

"You are arresting me?" Flinders asked.

"Not yet. Don't you want to talk business?"

The eyes of Milo Flinders flickered with surprise. "You mean—"

Steve smiled crookedly. "How much is it worth to you—to tear up this confession?"

Flinders sat still for a long time, studying Steve. Then he said, "I don't trust you, Klaw. I don't believe you'd sell out. You're not that kind of man."

Steve shrugged. He picked up the confession. "Then you don't want to talk business?"

"Wait!" Flinders raised a hand, "I suppose you know that confession is worthless. It was no doubt obtained under duress. You must have threatened Powers pretty effectively—to make him sign it."

"I'll say I did!" Steve grinned. "I turned on hot steam!"

"Then the confession would not even be admitted as evidence."

"But it could cause you a lot of trouble," Steve pointed out. "You might not be convicted—but it would break up your organization. It names a lot of names."

"So you want to sell it?" Flinders tapped his desk.

"Yes."

"And the price?"

"Your life!" said Stephen Klaw. "I'll give you a chance to get out from under—like a man. I'm going out of here now. Within twenty minutes, if you've committed suicide, I'll tear up this confession and your name will remain untarnished. If you're still alive, I'll take the confession to the Federal Attorney!"

Slowly, he put the confession in his pocket. Then he turned and walked toward the door.

MILO FLINDERS opened a drawer of his desk. From it he took a .32 caliber automatic pistol. He raised it, and aimed at Steve's back. "Klaw," he said, "you are a fool. This is your Last Mile!"

He pulled the trigger.

The shot struck Stephen Klaw square in the back, over the

heart. He stumbled forward, struck the wall, and slid down to the floor. His face became white, and his body twitched convulsively. Then he lay still.

Milo Flinders smiled. He pressed a button at the side of his desk, and when the door opened, he said casually, "Pim, you'll have to get rid of that body. I had to kill him...."

He stopped talking, and his mouth dropped open. Instead of his two bodyguards, Kerrigan and Murdoch stood in the doorway.

Neither said a word.

With a desperate motion, Milo Flinders raised the automatic. But he never pulled the trigger. For the guns of Kerrigan and Murdoch belched from the doorway. Lead smashed into the body of Milo Flinders with deadly accuracy. Thunder filled the room as Flinders went backward, crashed into the desk, then dropped inertly to the floor, blood gushing from his forehead and throat.

Kerrigan and Murdoch never gave him a second glance. They sprang to the side of the prone Stephen Klaw.

"He's dead!" sobbed Johnny Kerrigan. "I told him not to turn his back on Flinders, but no—he had to do it that way or not at all. And now look at him—he's dead!"

"Like hell I am!" said Stephen Klaw, and rolled over on his back.

He opened his coat to expose the leaded, bullet-proof vest he was wearing underneath it.

Murdoch blinked. "It worked then! I was afraid Flinders had shot you in the back of the head instead of going for the heart."

"No, he shot for the heart. And the slug fairly knocked me out for a minute. I can't catch my breath yet!"

Klaw grinned.

They helped him to his feet, and he straightened with difficulty. "I didn't think a thirty-two would carry such a wallop. But he fired from ten feet away." He looked somberly at the body of Milo Flinders. "Well, Flinders fell for the bait, he was suspicious, but I was sure he'd never let me walk out with that confession."

His partners nodded.

"We took the two bodyguards without much trouble," said Johnny Kerrigan. "And the butler too. But then we almost broke in before he shot you. We were afraid the vest wouldn't keep the slug out."

"But it did," said Stephen Klaw. He winked. "Okay, Mopes. Let's go report to the Director for our assignment in Chicago. Two to one he gives us a ten-day furlough."

"Or," said Johnny Kerrigan, "another case. Me, I'd like a case with some *real* action!"

POPULAR HERO PULPS AVAILABLE NOW:

THE SPIDER
- ❏ #1: The Spider Strikes — $13.95
- ❏ #2: The Wheel of Death — $13.95
- ❏ #3: Wings of the Black Death — $13.95
- ❏ #4: City of Flaming Shadows — $13.95
- ❏ #5: Empire of Doom! — $13.95
- ❏ #6: Citadel of Hell — $13.95
- ❏ #7: The Serpent of Destruction — $13.95
- ❏ #8: The Mad Horde — $13.95
- ❏ #9: Satan's Death Blast — $13.95
- ❏ #10: The Corpse Cargo — $13.95
- ❏ #11: Prince of the Red Looters — $13.95
- ❏ #12: Reign of the Silver Terror — $13.95
- ❏ #13: Builders of the Dark Empire — $13.95
- ❏ #14: Death's Crimson Juggernaut — $13.95
- ❏ #15: The Red Death Rain — $13.95
- ❏ #16: The City Destroyer — $13.95
- ❏ #17: The Pain Emperor — $13.95
- ❏ #18: The Flame Master — $13.95
- ❏ #19: Slaves of the Crime Master — $13.95
- ❏ #20: Reign of the Death Fiddler — $13.95
- ❏ #21: Hordes of the Red Butcher — $13.95
- ❏ #22: Dragon Lord of the Underworld — $13.95
- ❏ #23: Master of the Death-Madness — $13.95
- ❏ #24: King of the Red Killers — $13.95
- ❏ #25: Overlord of the Damned — $13.95
- ❏ #26: Death Reign of the Vampire King — $13.95
- ❏ #27: Emperor of the Yellow Death — $13.95
- ❏ #28: The Mayor of Hell — $13.95
- ❏ #29: Slaves of the Murder Syndicate — $13.95
- ❏ #30: Green Globes of Death — $13.95
- ❏ #31: The Cholera King — $13.95
- ❏ #32: Slaves of the Dragon — $13.95
- ❏ #33: Legions of Madness — $12.95
- ❏ #34: Laboratory of the Damned — $12.95
- ❏ #35: Satan's Sightless Legion — $12.95
- ❏ #36: The Coming of the Terror — $12.95
- ❏ #37: The Devil's Death-Dwarfs — $12.95
- ❏ #38: City of Dreadful Night — $12.95
- ❏ #39: Reign of the Snake Men — $12.95
- ❏ #40: Dictator of the Damned — $12.95
- ❏ #41: The Mill-Town Massacres — $12.95
- ❏ #42: Satan's Workshop — $12.95
- ❏ #43: Scourge of the Yellow Fangs — $12.95
- ❏ #44: The Devil's Pawnbroker — $12.95
- ❏ #45: Voyage of the Coffin Ship — $12.95
- ❏ #46: The Man Who Ruled in Hell — $13.95
- ❏ #47: Slaves of the Black Monarch — $13.95
- ❏ #48: Machineguns Over the White House — $13.95
- ❏ #49: The City That Dared Not Eat — $13.95
- ❏ #50: Master of the Flaming Horde — $13.95
- ❏ #51: Satan's Switchboard — $13.95
- ❏ #52: Legions of the Accursed Light — $13.95
- ❏ #53: The City of Lost Men — $13.95
- ❏ #54: The Grey Horde Creeps — $13.95
- ❏ #55: City of Whispering Death — $13.95
- ❏ #56: When Thousands Slept in Hell — $13.95
- ❏ #57: Satan's Shakles — $14.95
- ❏ **NEW:** #58: The Emperor From Hell — $14.95

THE WESTERN RAIDER
- ❏ #1: Guns of the Damned — $13.95
- ❏ #2: The Hawk Rides Back from Death — $13.95
- ❏ #3: Gun-Call for the Lost Legion — $13.95
- ❏ #4: The Law of Silver Trent — $13.95
- ❏ #5: The Gun-Prayer of Silver Trent — $13.95
- ❏ #6: Silver Trent Rides Alone — $13.95

G-8 AND HIS BATTLE ACES
- ❏ #1: The Bat Staffel — $13.95

CAPTAIN SATAN
- ❏ #1: The Mask of the Damned — $13.95
- ❏ #2: Parole for the Dead — $13.95
- ❏ #3: The Dead Man Express — $13.95
- ❏ #4: A Ghost Rides the Dawn — $13.95
- ❏ #5: The Ambassador From Hell — $13.95

DR. YEN SIN
- ❏ #1: Mystery of the Dragon's Shadow — $12.95
- ❏ #2: Mystery of the Golden Skull — $12.95
- ❏ #3: Mystery of the Singing Mummies — $12.95

POPULAR HERO PULPS AVAILABLE NOW:

ACE G-MAN
- ❏ #1: The Suicide Squad Reports for Death $14.95

CAPTAIN COMBAT
- ❏ #1: The Sky Beast of Berlin $13.95
- ❏ #2: Red Wings For the Blood Battalion $13.95
- ❏ #3: Low Ceiling For Nazi Hell Hawks $13.95

OPERATOR 5
- ❏ #1: The Masked Invasion $13.95
- ❏ #2: The Invisible Empire $13.95
- ❏ #3: The Yellow Scourge $13.95
- ❏ #4: The Melting Death $13.95
- ❏ #5: Cavern of the Damned $13.95
- ❏ #6: Master of Broken Men $13.95
- ❏ #7: Invasion of the Dark Legions $13.95
- ❏ #8: The Green Death Mists $13.95
- ❏ #9: Legions of Starvation $13.95
- ❏ #10: The Red Invader $13.95
- ❏ #11: The League of War-Monsters $13.95
- ❏ #12: The Army of the Dead $13.95
- ❏ #13: March of the Flame Marauders $13.95
- ❏ #14: Blood Reign of the Dictator $13.95
- ❏ #15: Invasion of the Yellow Warlords $13.95
- ❏ #16: Legions of the Death Master $13.95
- ❏ #17: Hosts of the Flaming Death $13.95
- ❏ #18: Invasion of the Crimson Death Cult $13.95
- ❏ #19: Attack of the Blizzard Men $13.95
- ❏ #20: Scourge of the Invisible Death $13.95
- ❏ #21: Raiders of the Red Death $13.95
- ❏ #22: War-Dogs of the Green Destroyer $13.95
- ❏ #23: Rockets From Hell $13.95
- ❏ #24: War-Masters from the Orient $13.95
- ❏ #25: Crime's Reign of Terror $13.95
- ❏ #26: Death's Ragged Army $13.95
- ❏ #27: Patriots' Death Battalion $13.95
- ❏ #28: The Bloody Forty-five Days $13.95
- ❏ #29: America's Plague Battalions $13.95
- ❏ #30: Liberty's Suicide Legions $13.95
- ❏ #31: Siege of the Thousand Patriots $13.95
- ❏ #32: Patriots' Death March $14.95

DUSTY AYRES AND HIS BATTLE BIRDS
- ❏ #1: Black Lightning! $13.95
- ❏ #2: Crimson Doom $13.95
- ❏ #3: The Purple Tornado $13.95
- ❏ #4: The Screaming Eye $13.95
- ❏ #5: The Green Thunderbolt $13.95
- ❏ #6: The Red Destroyer $13.95
- ❏ #7: The White Death $13.95
- ❏ #8: The Black Avenger $13.95
- ❏ #9: The Silver Typhoon $13.95
- ❏ #10: The Troposphere F-S $13.95
- ❏ #11: The Blue Cyclone $13.95
- ❏ #12: The Tesla Raiders $13.95

MAVERICKS
- ❏ #1: Five Against the Law $12.95
- ❏ #2: Mesquite Manhunters $12.95
- ❏ #3: Bait for the Lobo Pack $12.95
- ❏ #4: Doc Grimson's Outlaw Posse $12.95
- ❏ #5: Charlie Parr's Gunsmoke Cure $12.95

THE MYSTERIOUS WU FANG
- ❏ #1: The Case of the Six Coffins $12.95
- ❏ #2: The Case of the Scarlet Feather $12.95
- ❏ #3: The Case of the Yellow Mask $12.95
- ❏ #4: The Case of the Suicide Tomb $12.95
- ❏ #5: The Case of the Green Death $12.95
- ❏ #6: The Case of the Black Lotus $12.95
- ❏ #7: The Case of the Hidden Scourge $12.95

THE SECRET 6
- ❏ #1: The Red Shadow $13.95
- ❏ #2: House of Walking Corpses $13.95
- ❏ #3: The Monster Murders $13.95
- ❏ #4: The Golden Alligator $13.95

CAPTAIN ZERO
- ❏ #1: City of Deadly Sleep $13.95
- ❏ #2: The Mark of Zero! $13.95
- ❏ #3: The Golden Murder Syndicate $13.95